THE SCHOOL

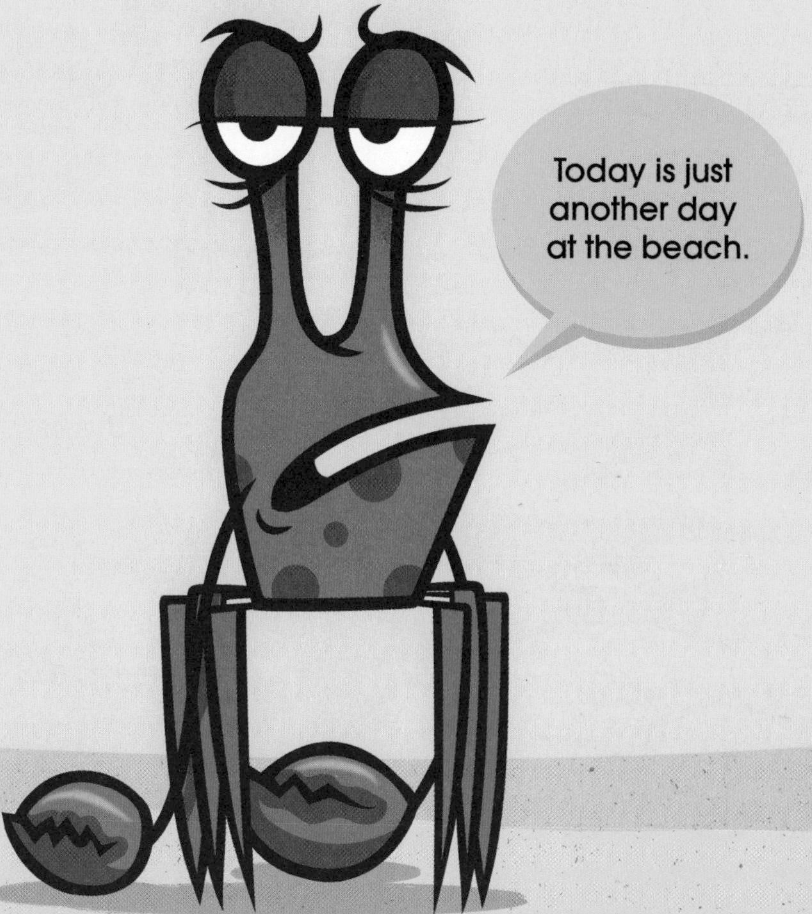
Today is just another day at the beach.

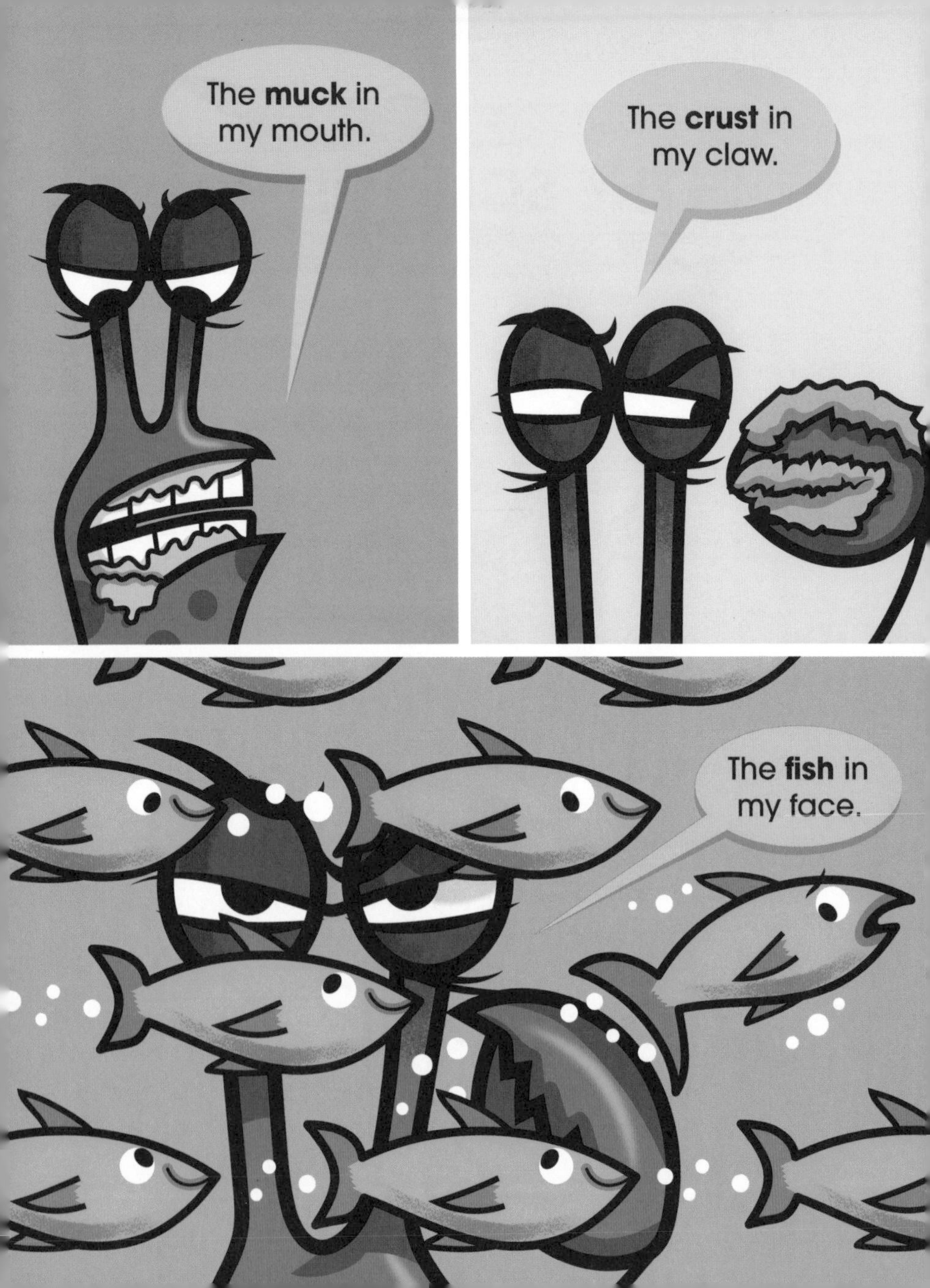
The **muck** in my mouth.
The **crust** in my claw.
The **fish** in my face.

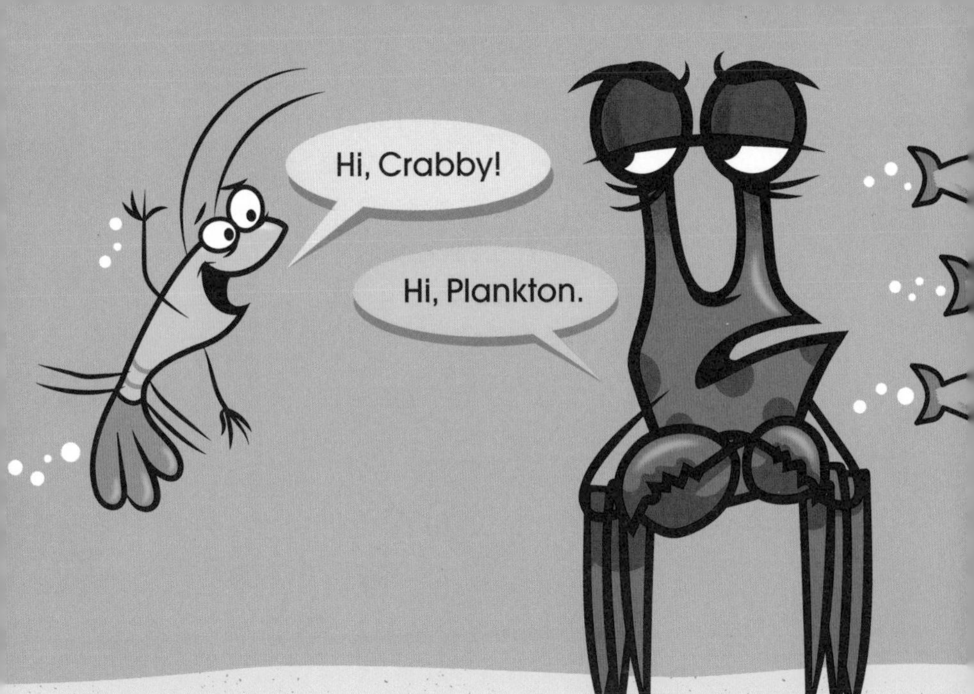
Hi, Crabby!
Hi, Plankton.

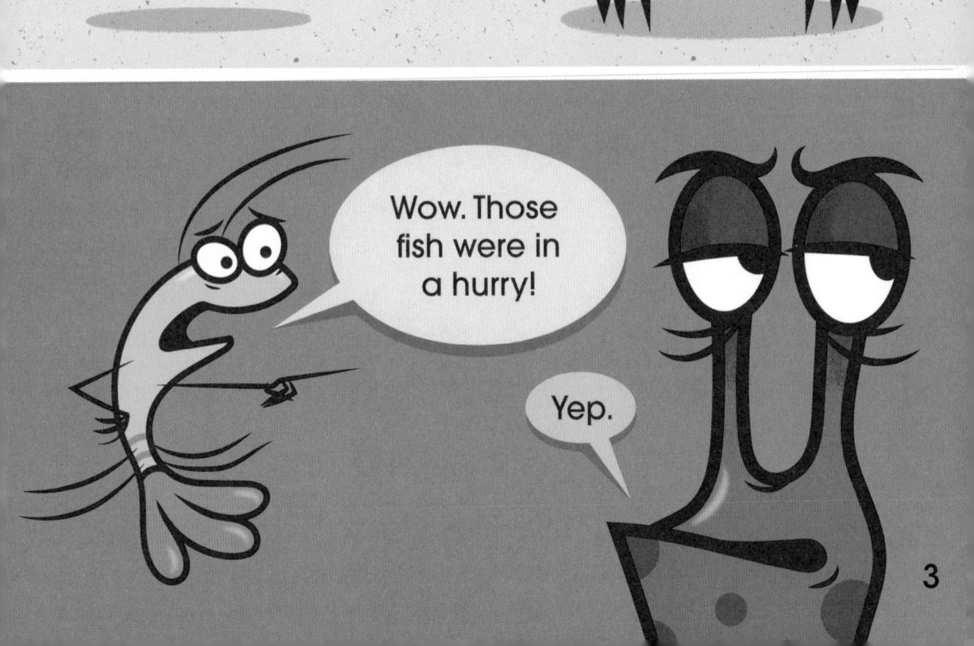
Wow. Those fish were in a hurry!
Yep.

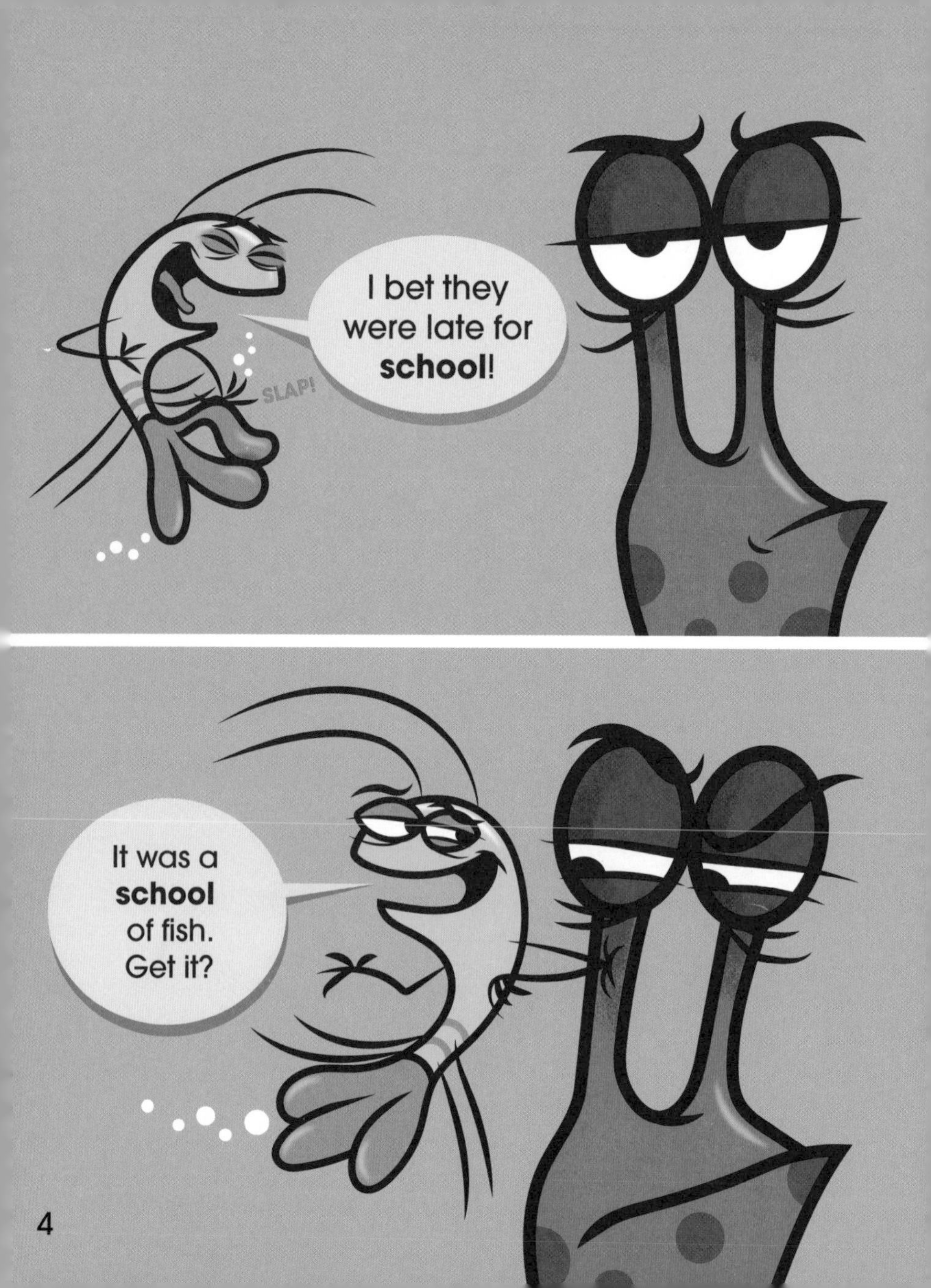
I bet they were late for **school**!
SLAP!
It was a **school** of fish. Get it?

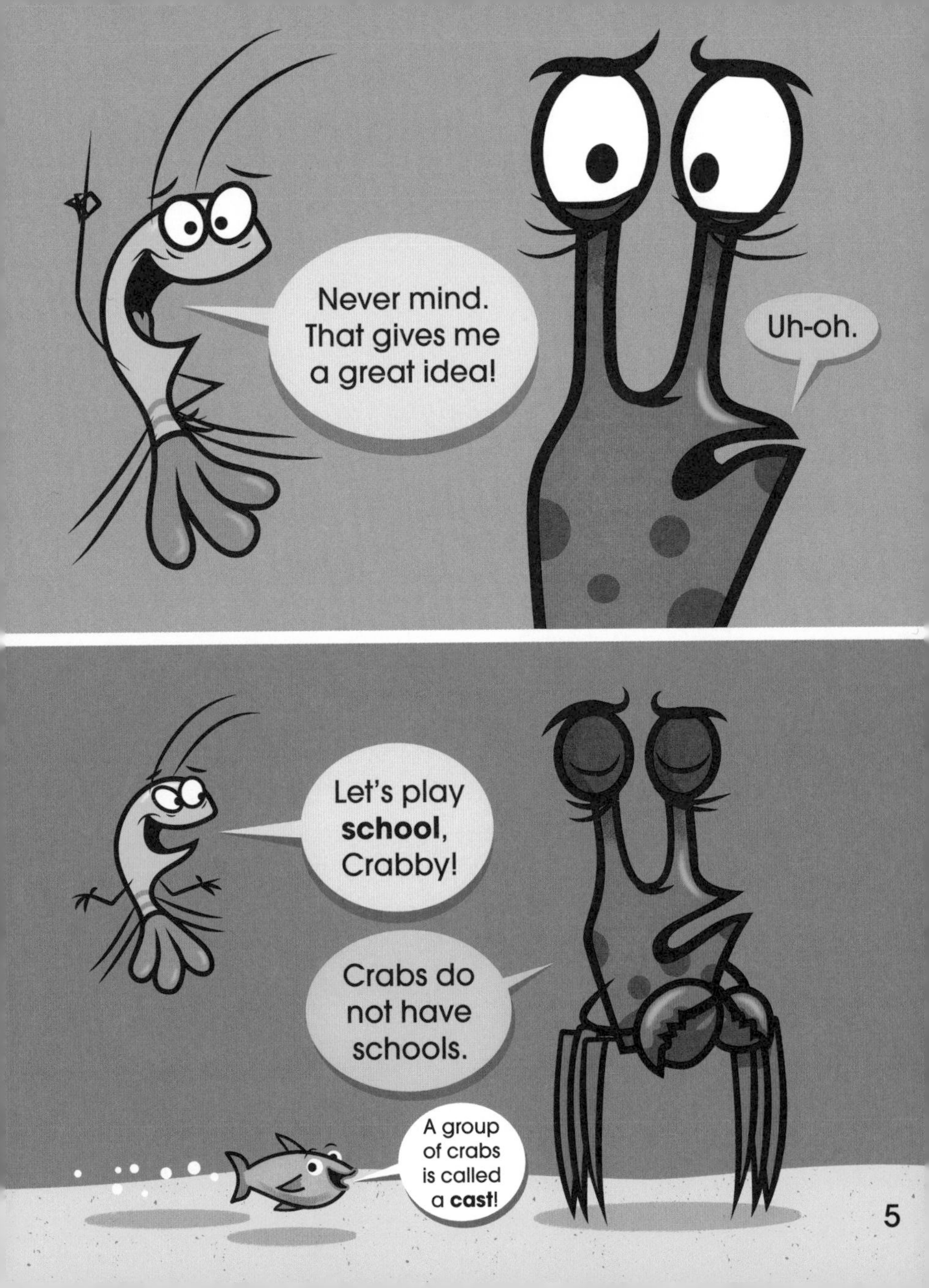
Never mind. That gives me a great idea!
Uh-oh.
Let's play **school**, Crabby!
Crabs do not have schools.
A group of crabs is called a **cast**!

6

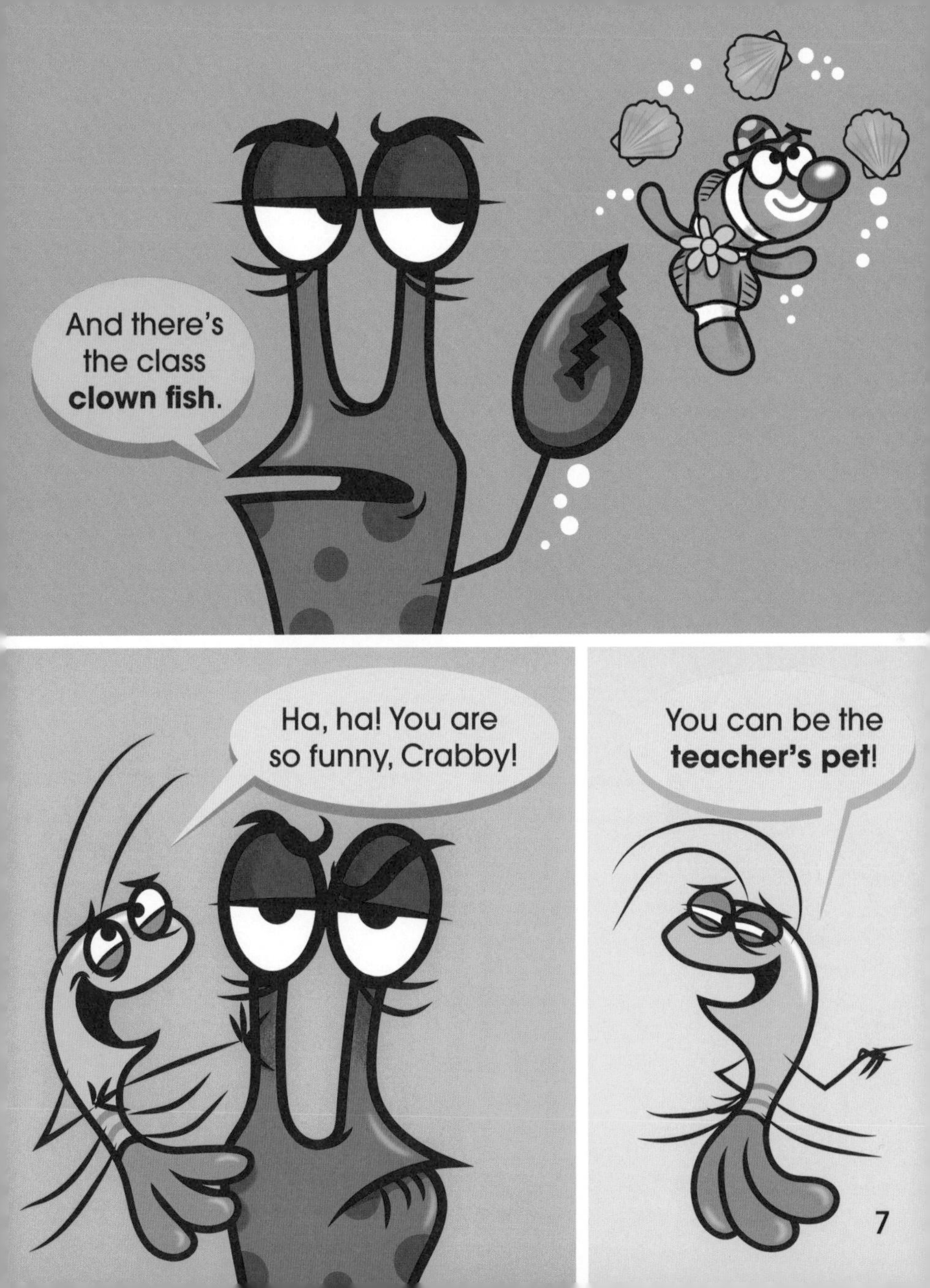
And there's the class **clown fish**.
Ha, ha! You are so funny, Crabby!
You can be the **teacher's pet**!

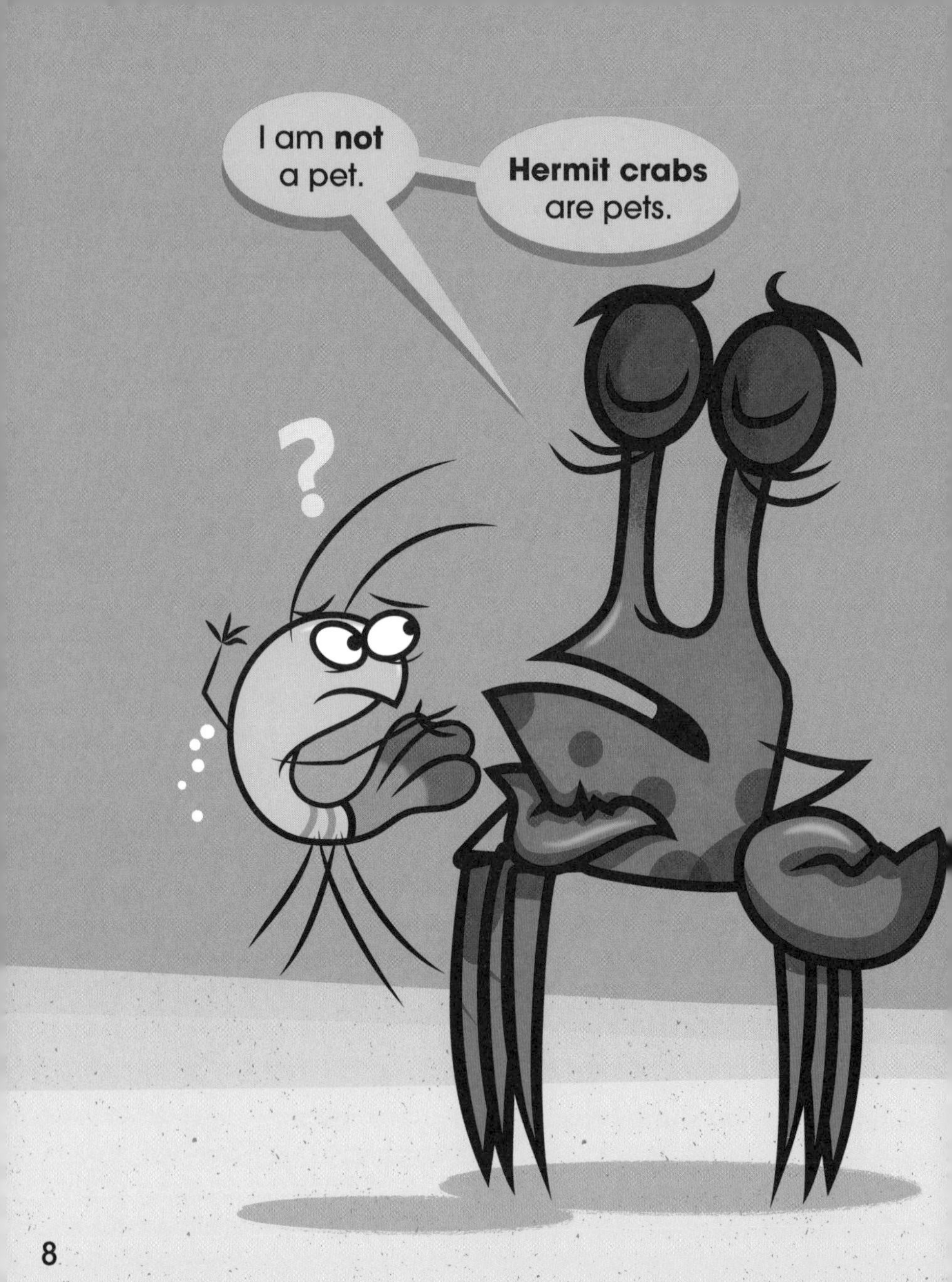
I am **not** a pet.
Hermit crabs are pets.
?

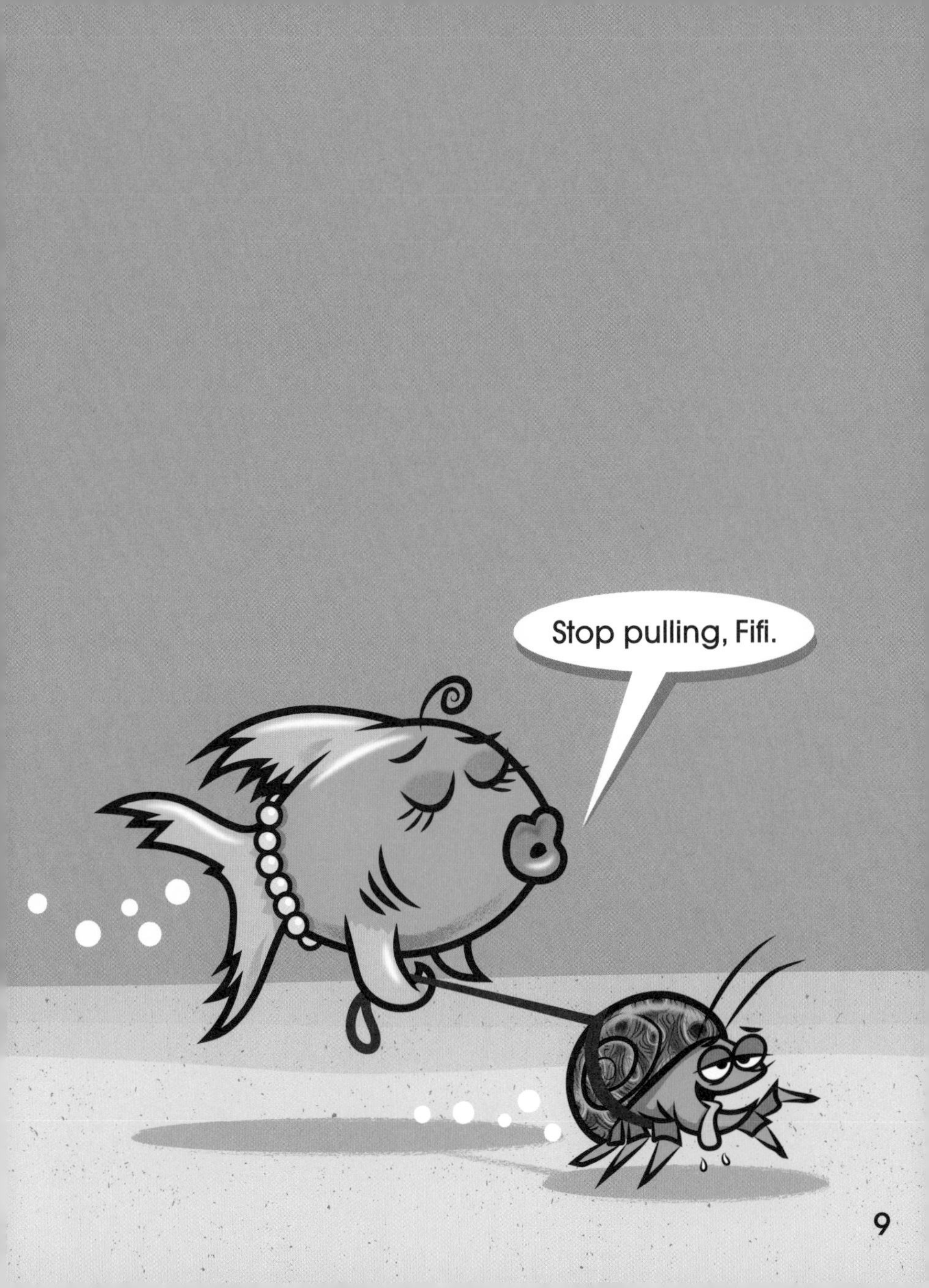
Stop pulling, Fifi.

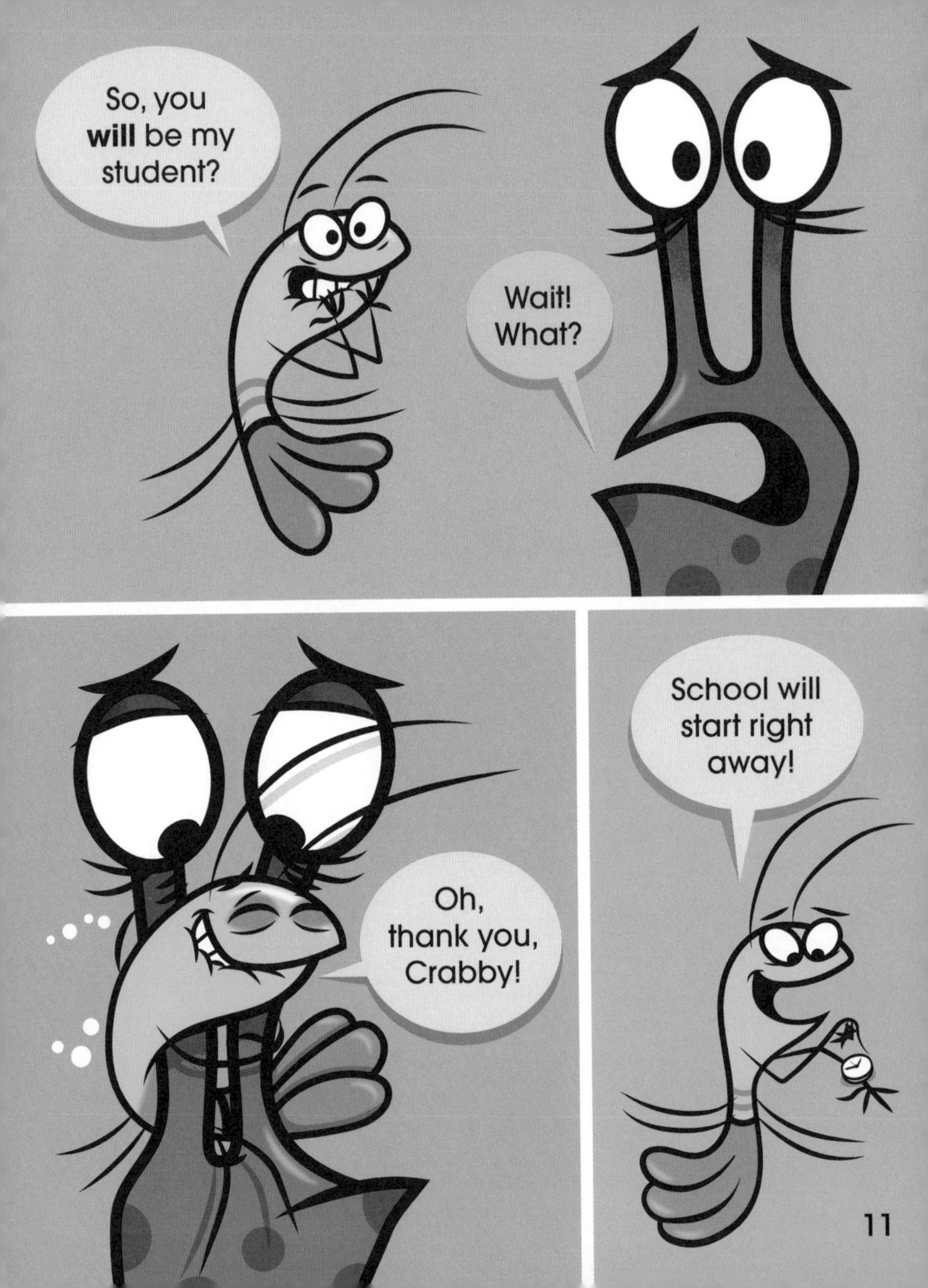
So, you **will** be my student?
Wait! What?
Oh, thank you, Crabby!
School will start right away!

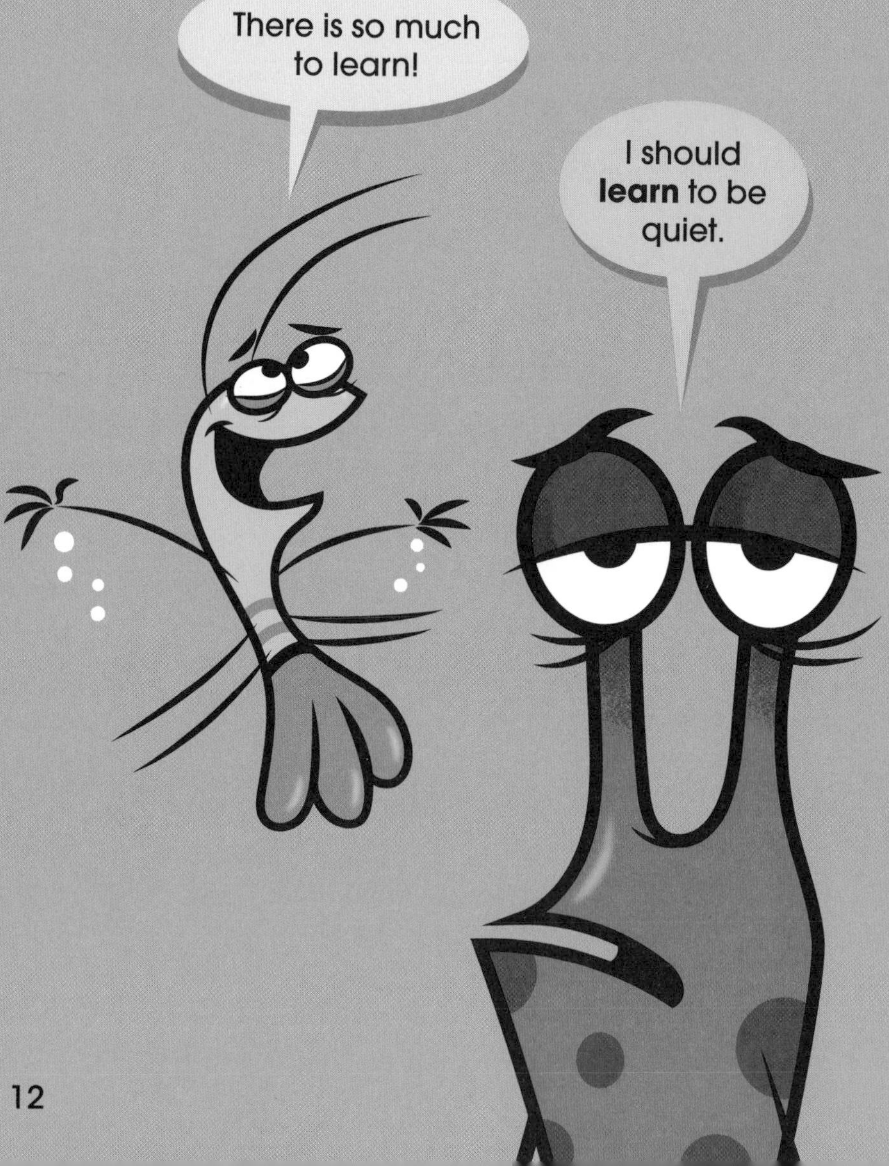
There is so much to learn!
I should **learn** to be quiet.

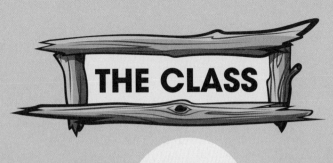

THE CLASS

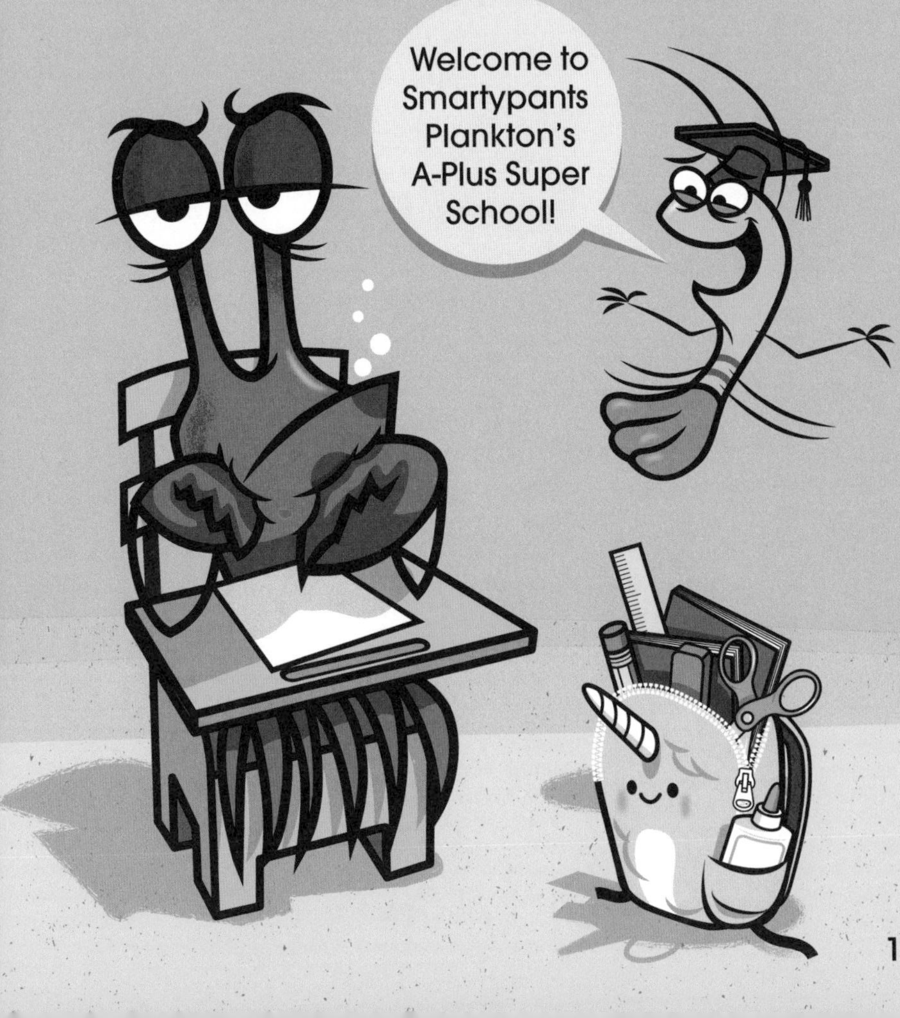
Welcome to Smartypants Plankton's A-Plus Super School!

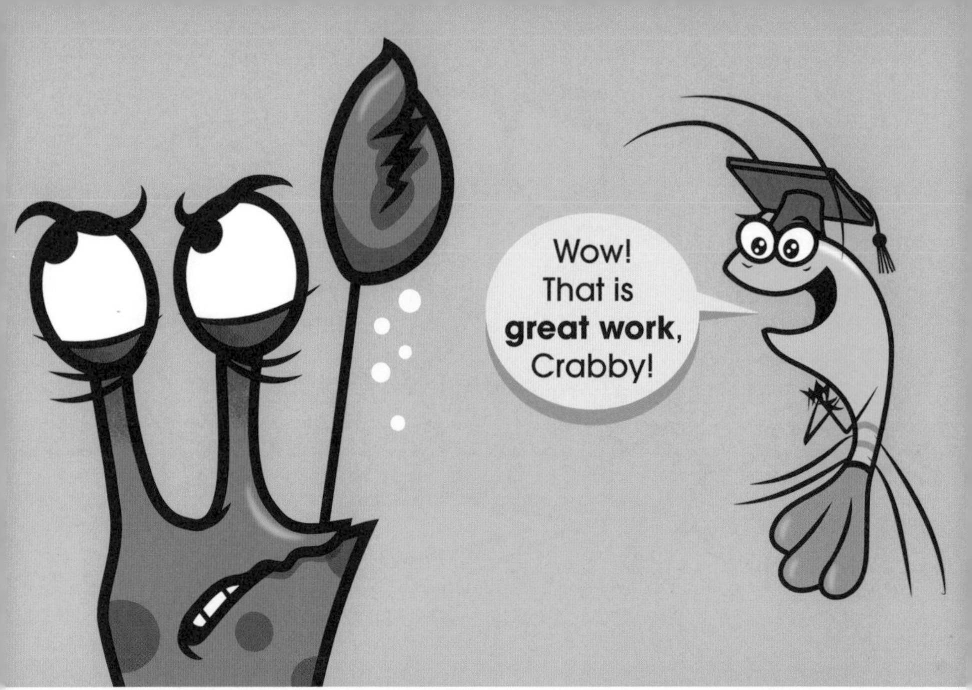
Wow! That is **great work,** Crabby!

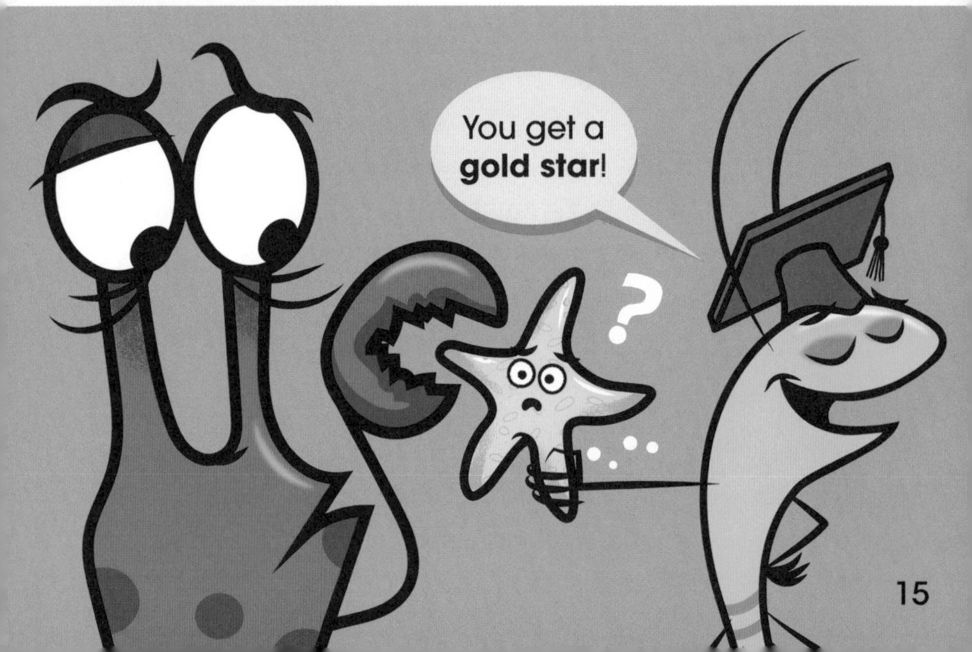
You get a **gold star**!
?

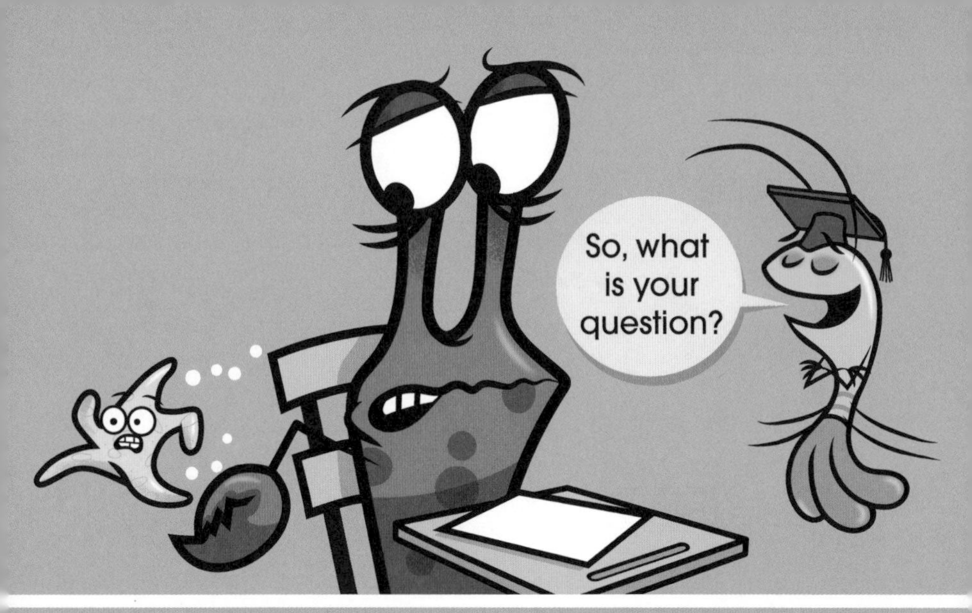
So, what is your question?

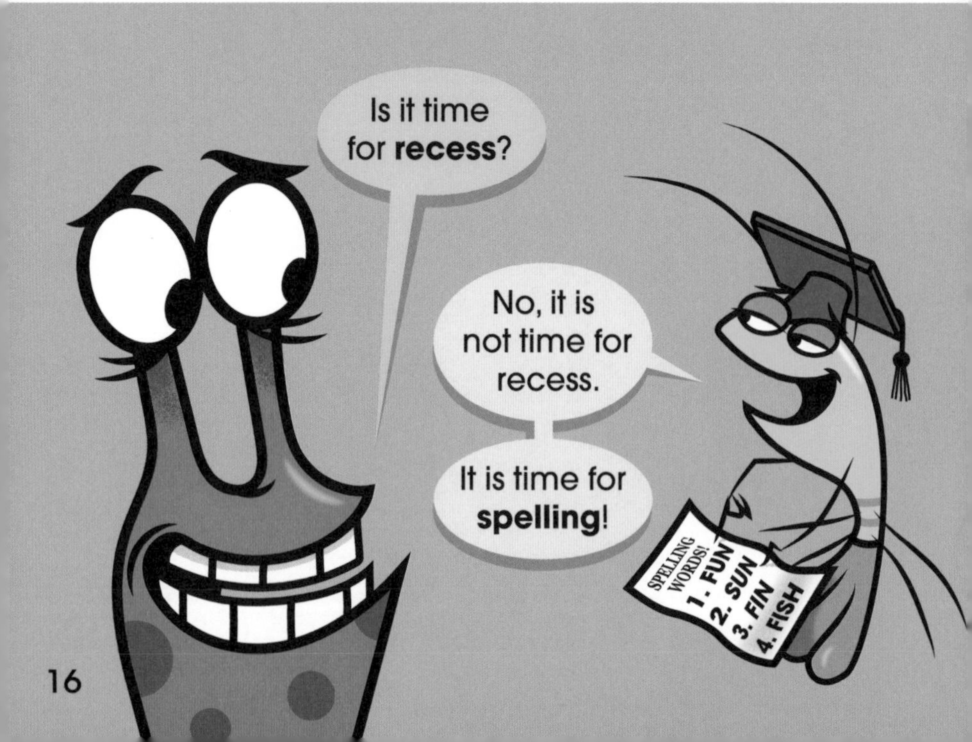
Is it time for **recess**?
No, it is not time for recess.
It is time for **spelling**!
SPELLING WORDS!
1. FUN
2. SUN
3. FIN
4. FISH

17

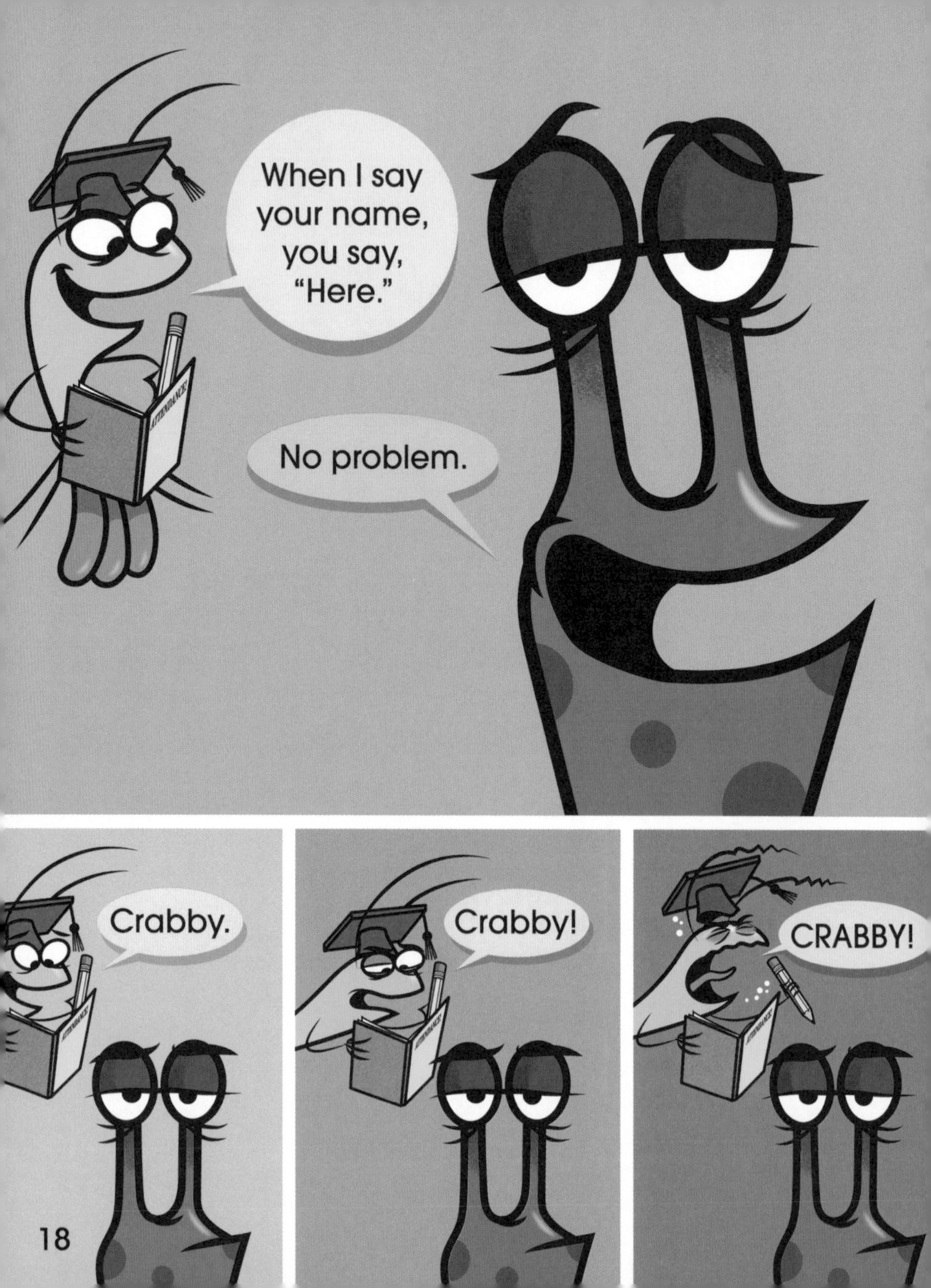
When I say your name, you say, "Here."
No problem.
Crabby.
Crabby!
CRABBY!

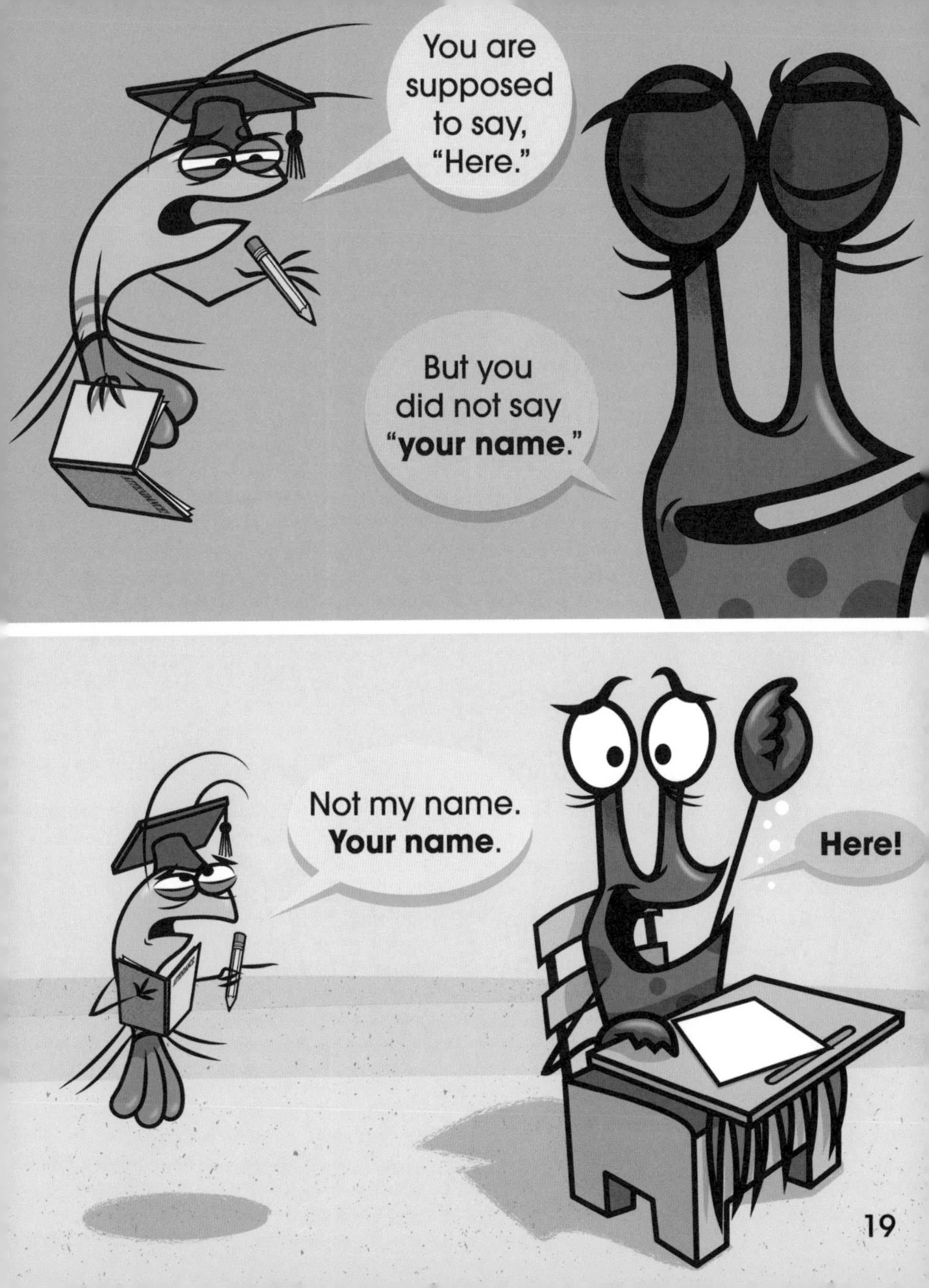
You are supposed to say, "Here."
But you did not say "**your name**."
Not my name. **Your name.**
Here!

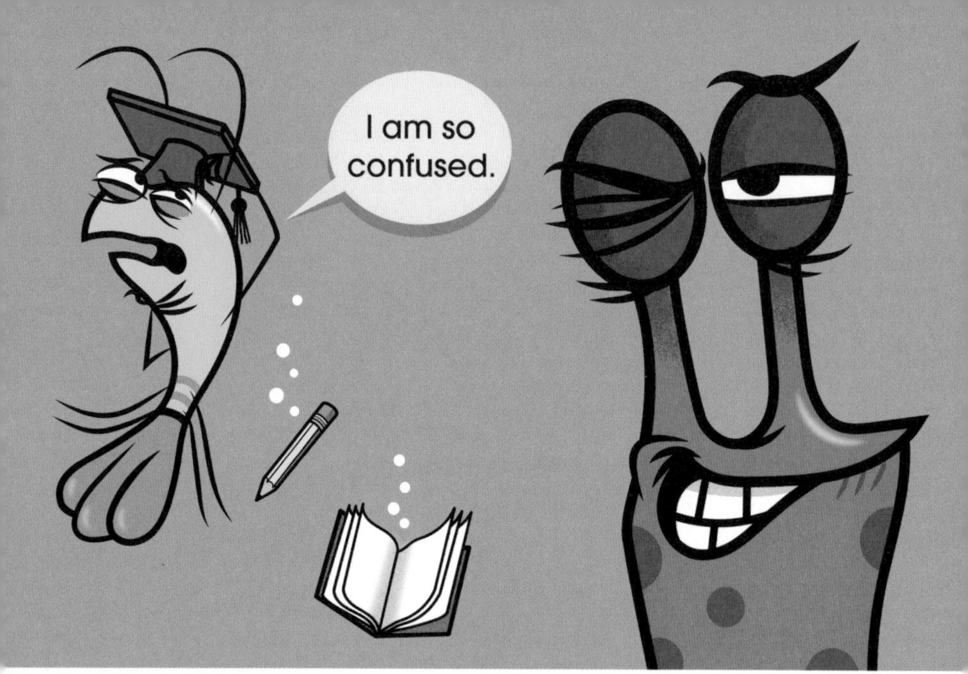
I am so confused.

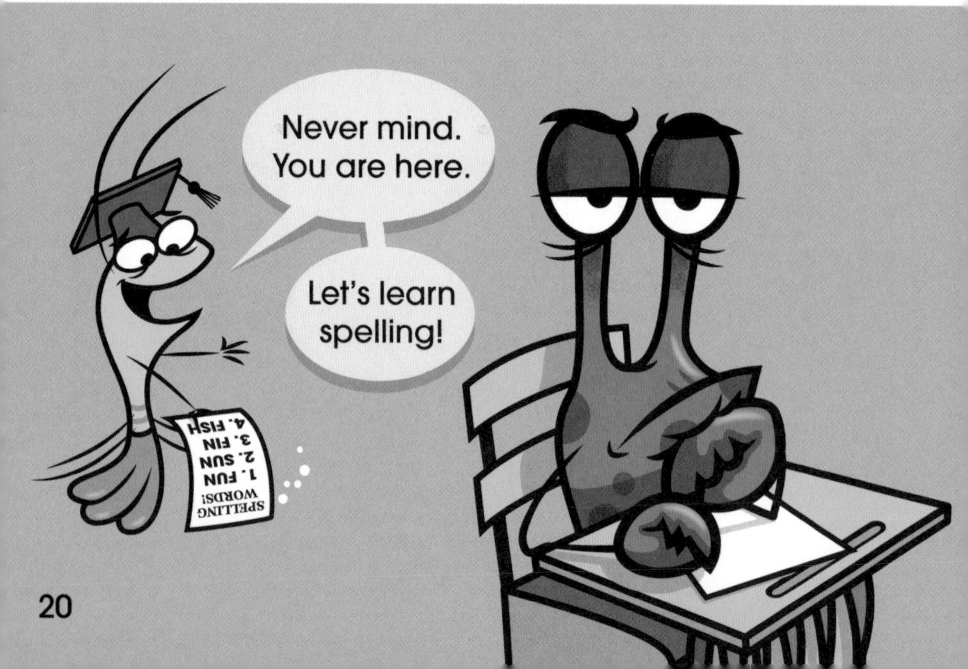
Never mind. You are here.
Let's learn spelling!
SPELLING WORDS!
1. FUN
2. SUN
3. FIN
4. FISH

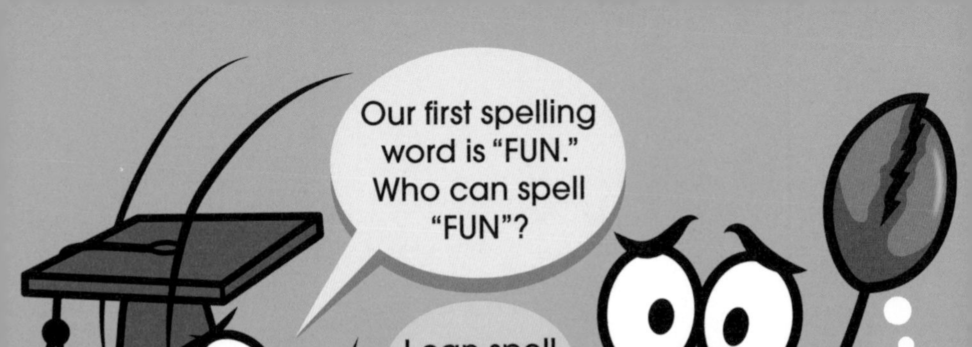
Our first spelling word is "FUN." Who can spell "FUN"?
I can spell "FUN"!
SPELLING WORDS!
1. FUN
2. SUN
3. FIN
4. FISH

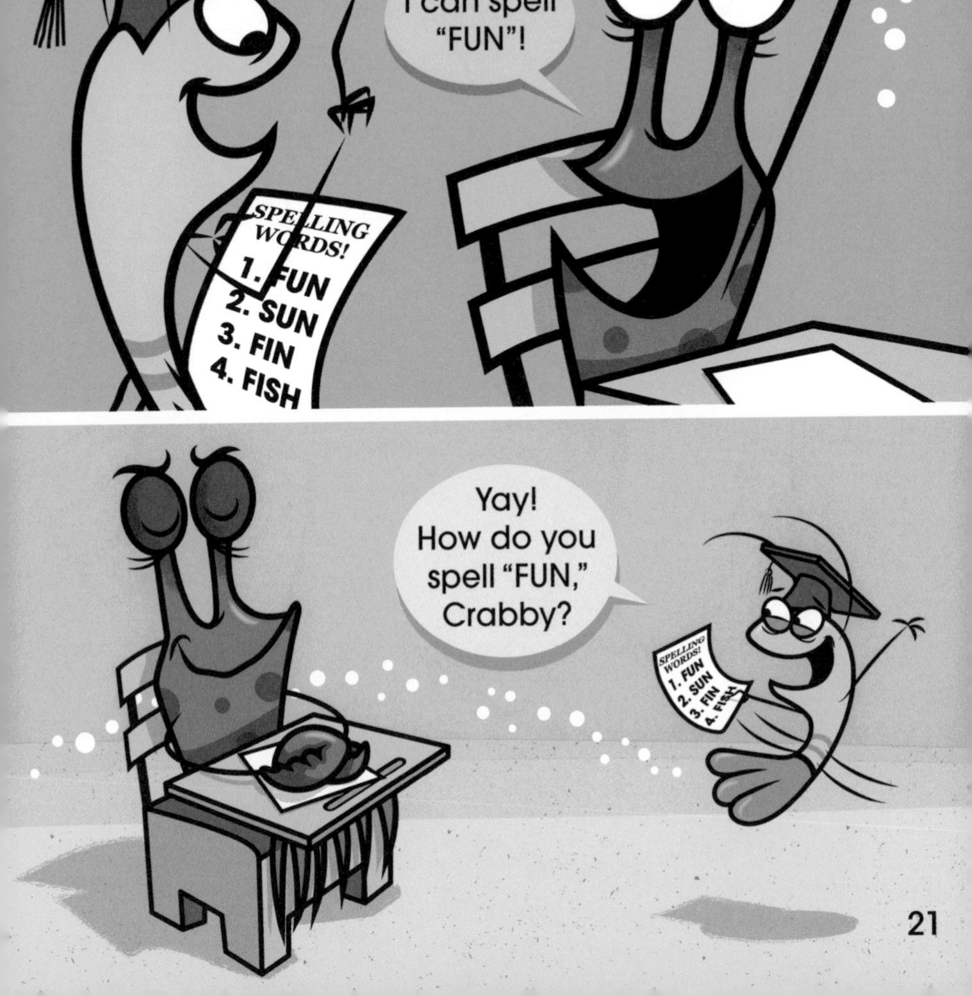
Yay! How do you spell "FUN," Crabby?

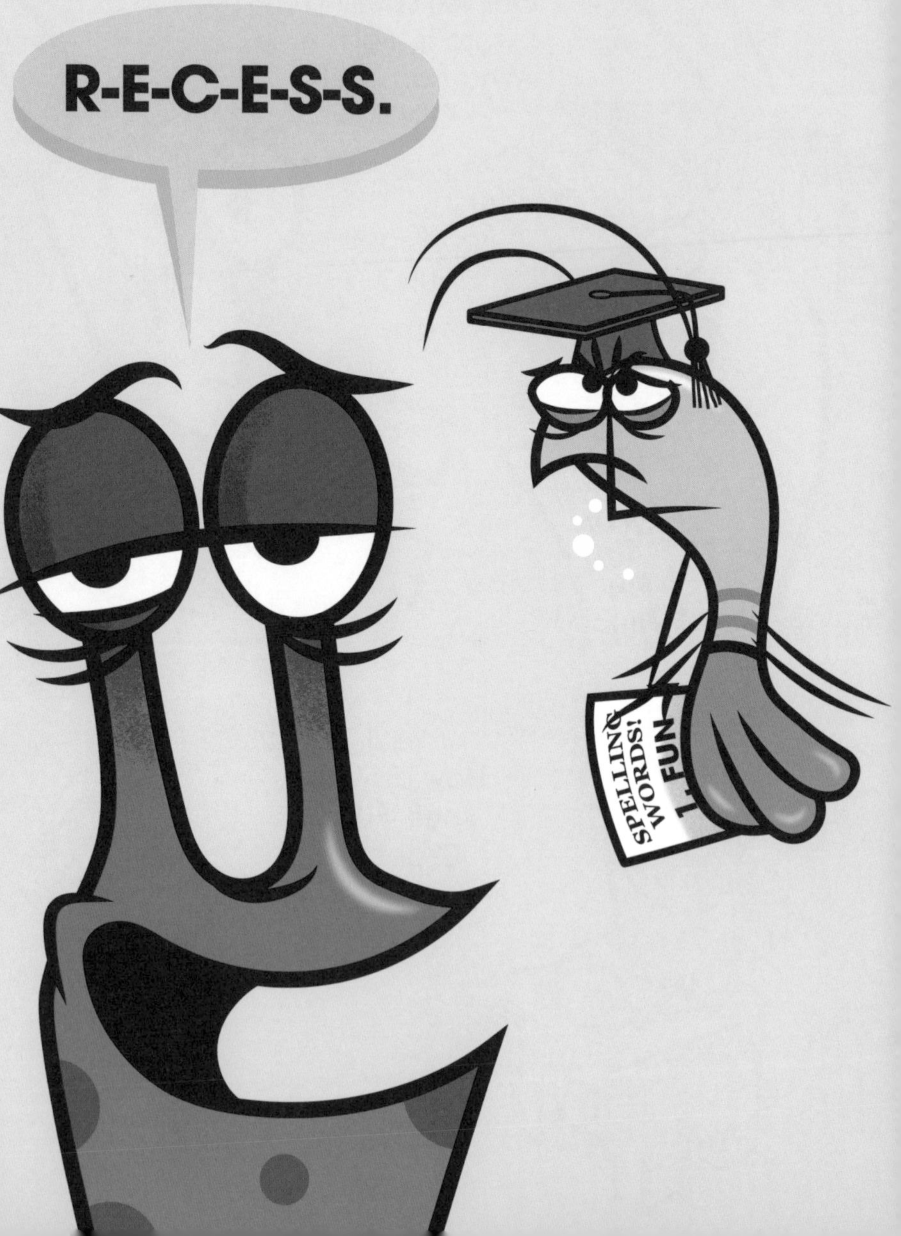
R-E-C-E-S-S.
SPELLING WORDS!
1. FUN

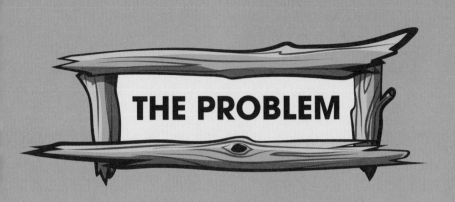

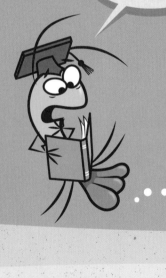

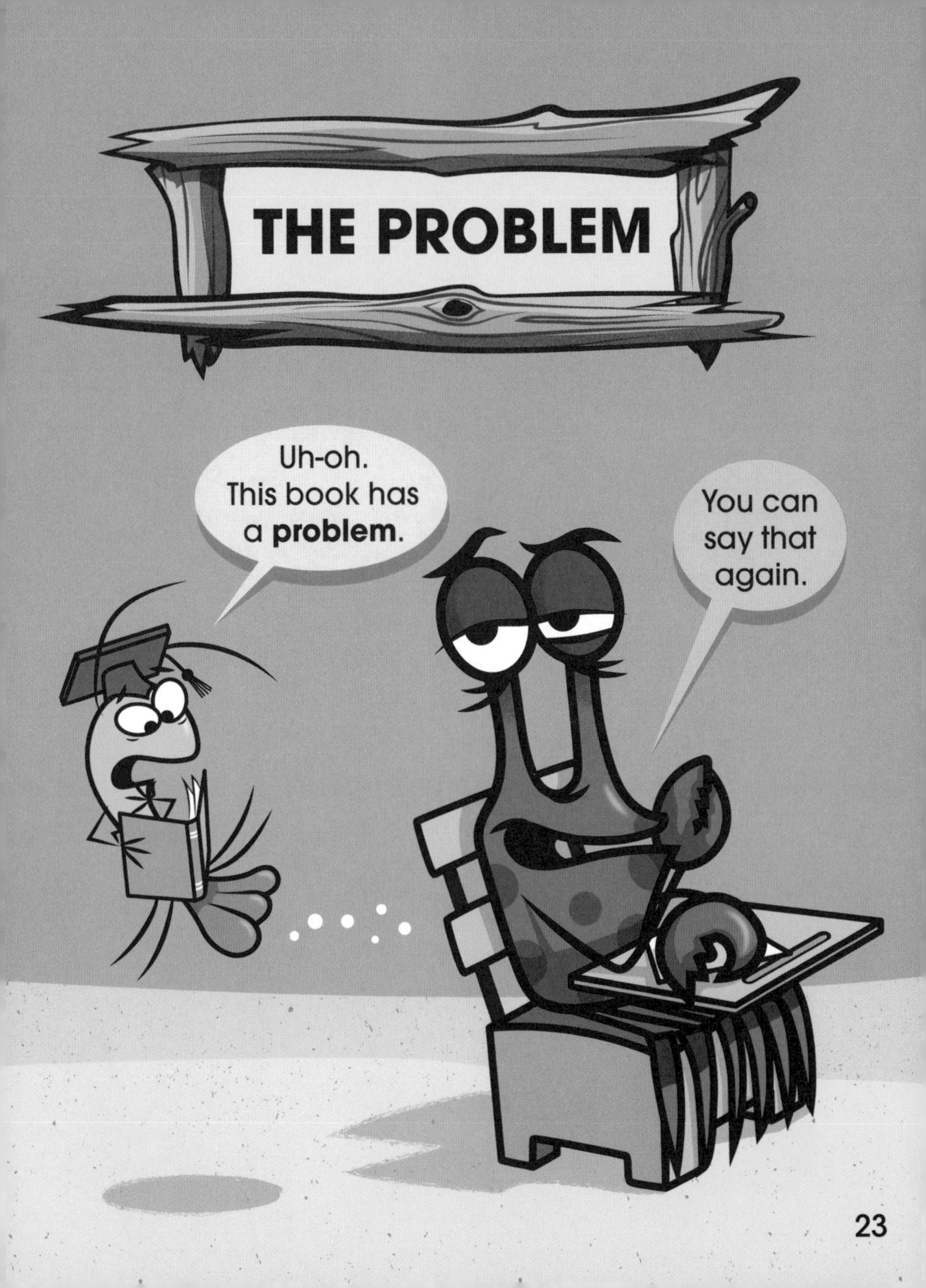
THE PROBLEM
Uh-oh.
This book has
a **problem**.
You can
say that
again.

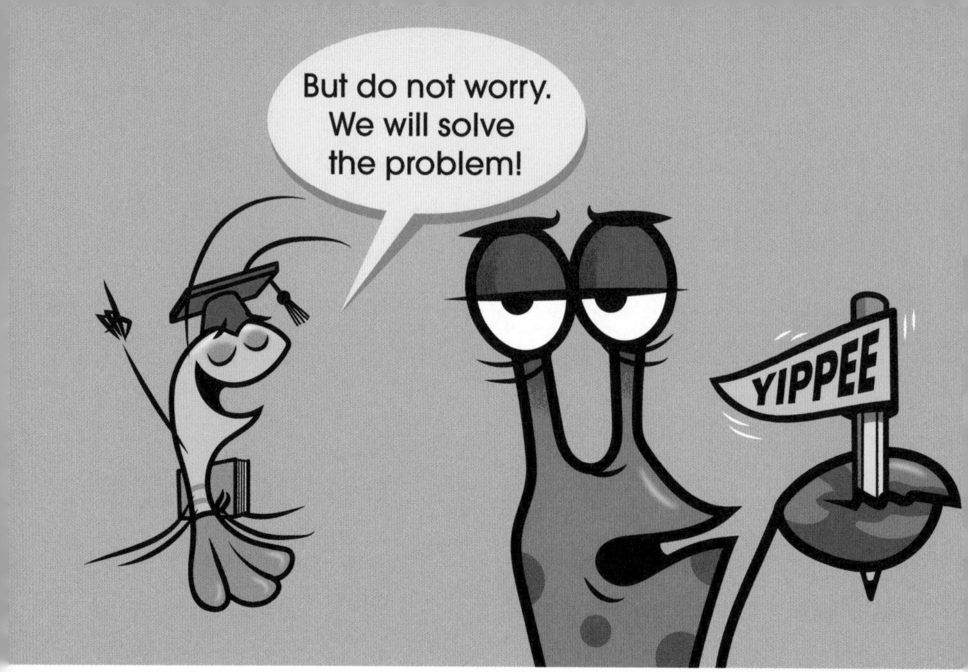
But do not worry. We will solve the problem!
YIPPEE

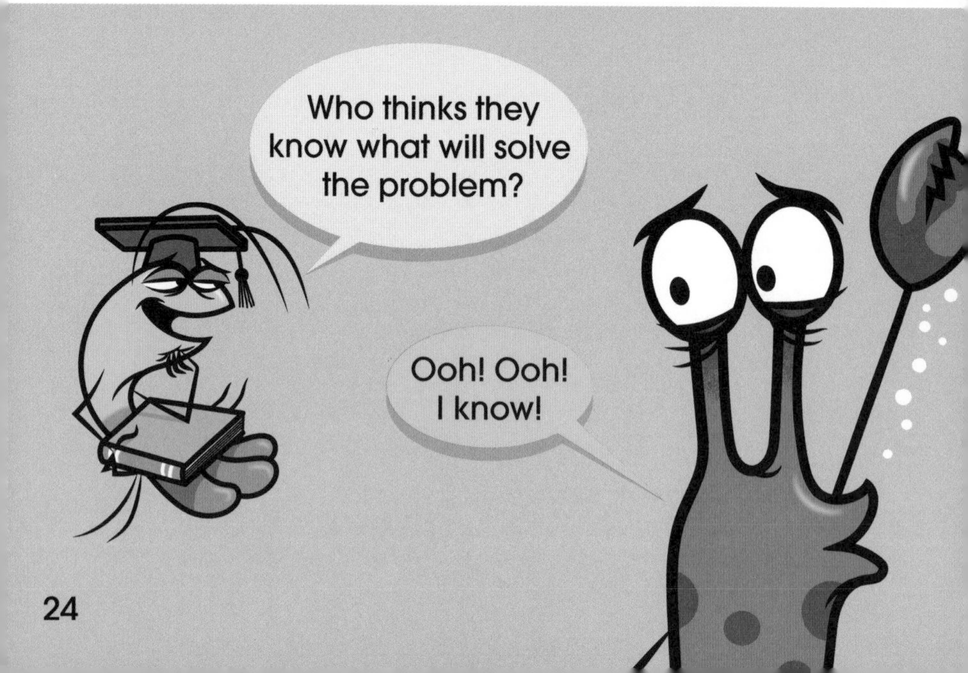
Who thinks they know what will solve the problem?
Ooh! Ooh! I know!

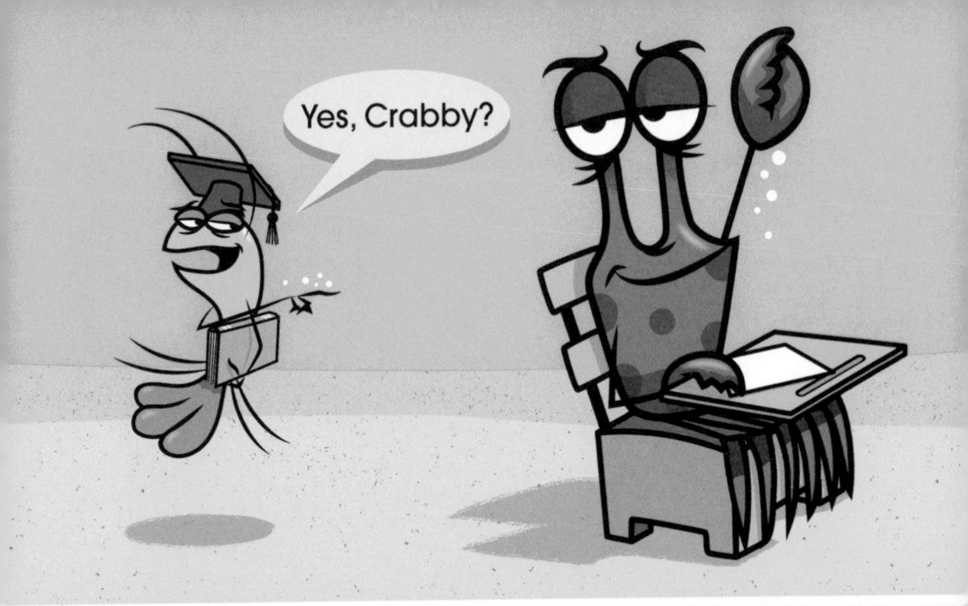
Yes, Crabby?

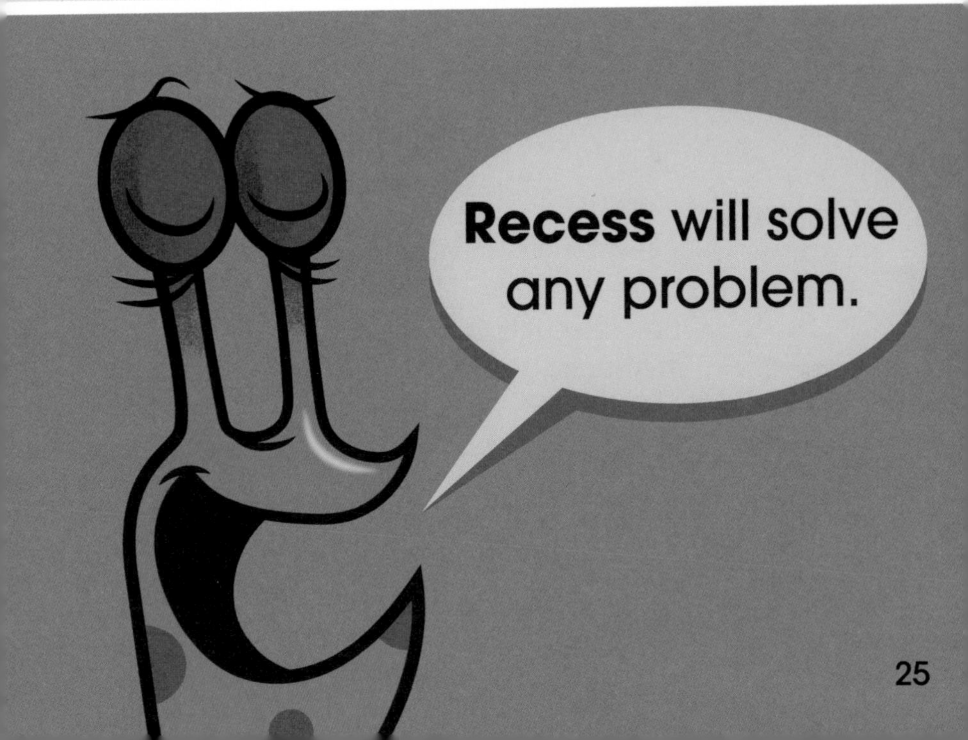
Recess will solve any problem.

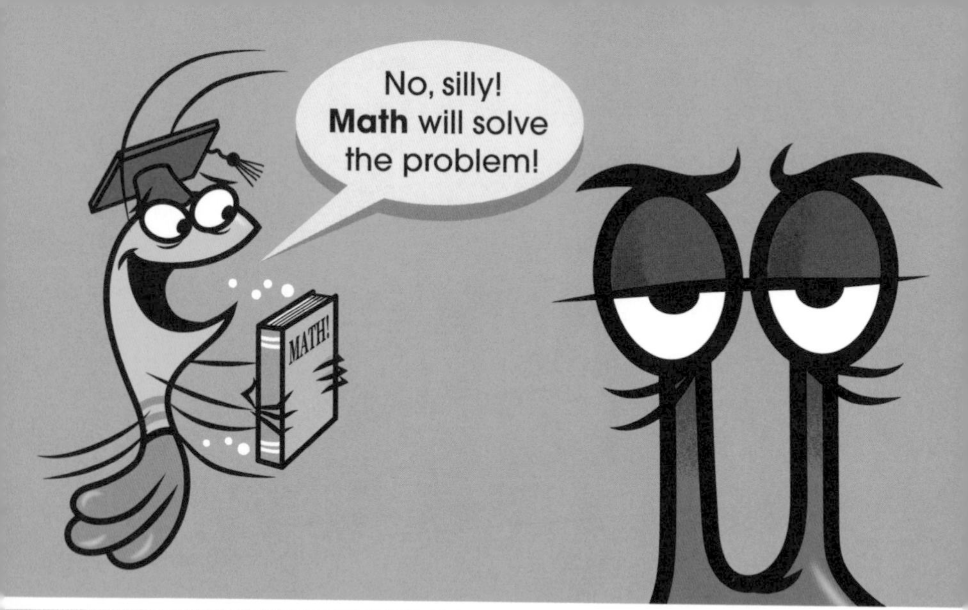
No, silly! **Math** will solve the problem!
MATH!

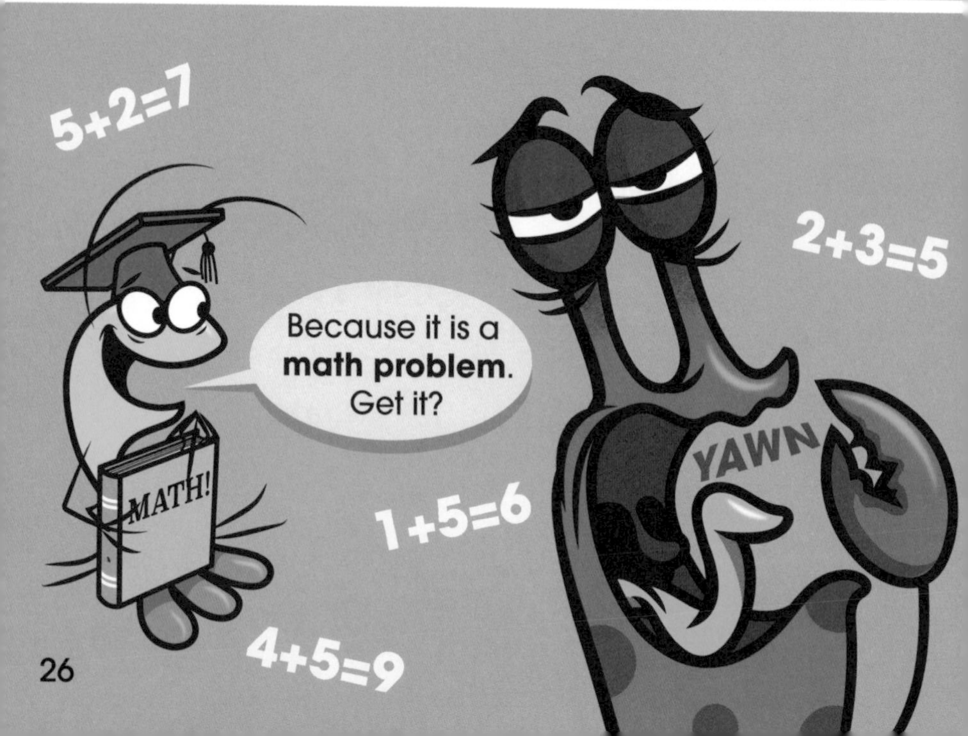
5+2=7
2+3=5
Because it is a **math problem**. Get it?
MATH!
YAWN
1+5=6
4+5=9

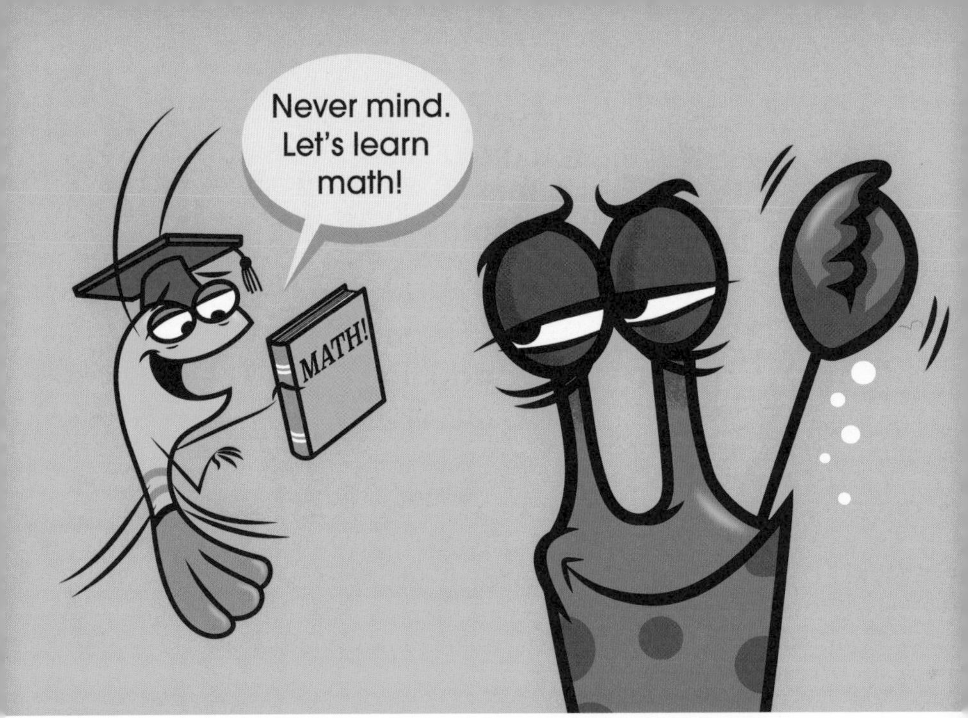
Never mind. Let's learn math!
MATH!

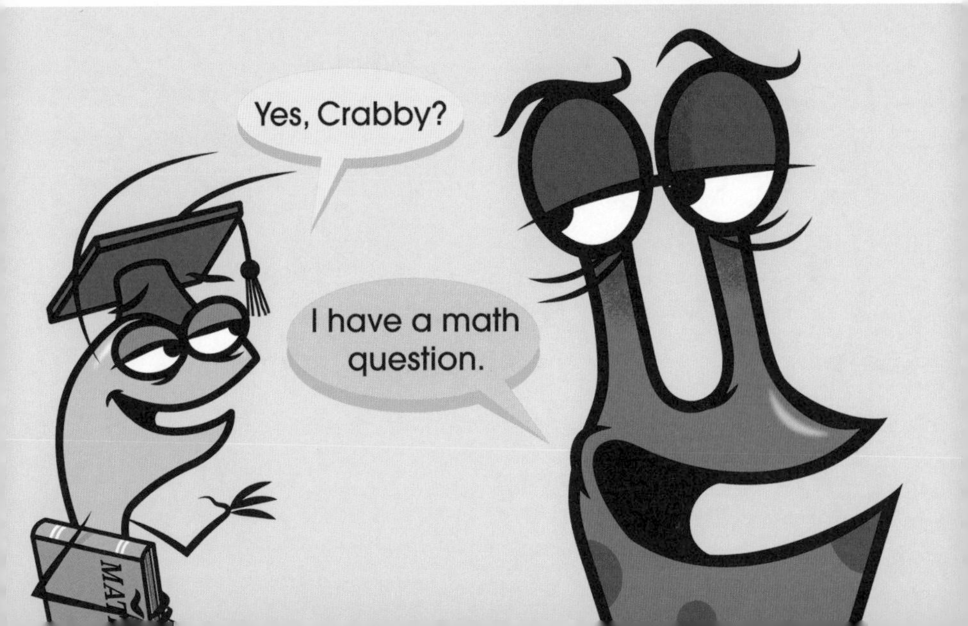
Yes, Crabby?
I have a math question.

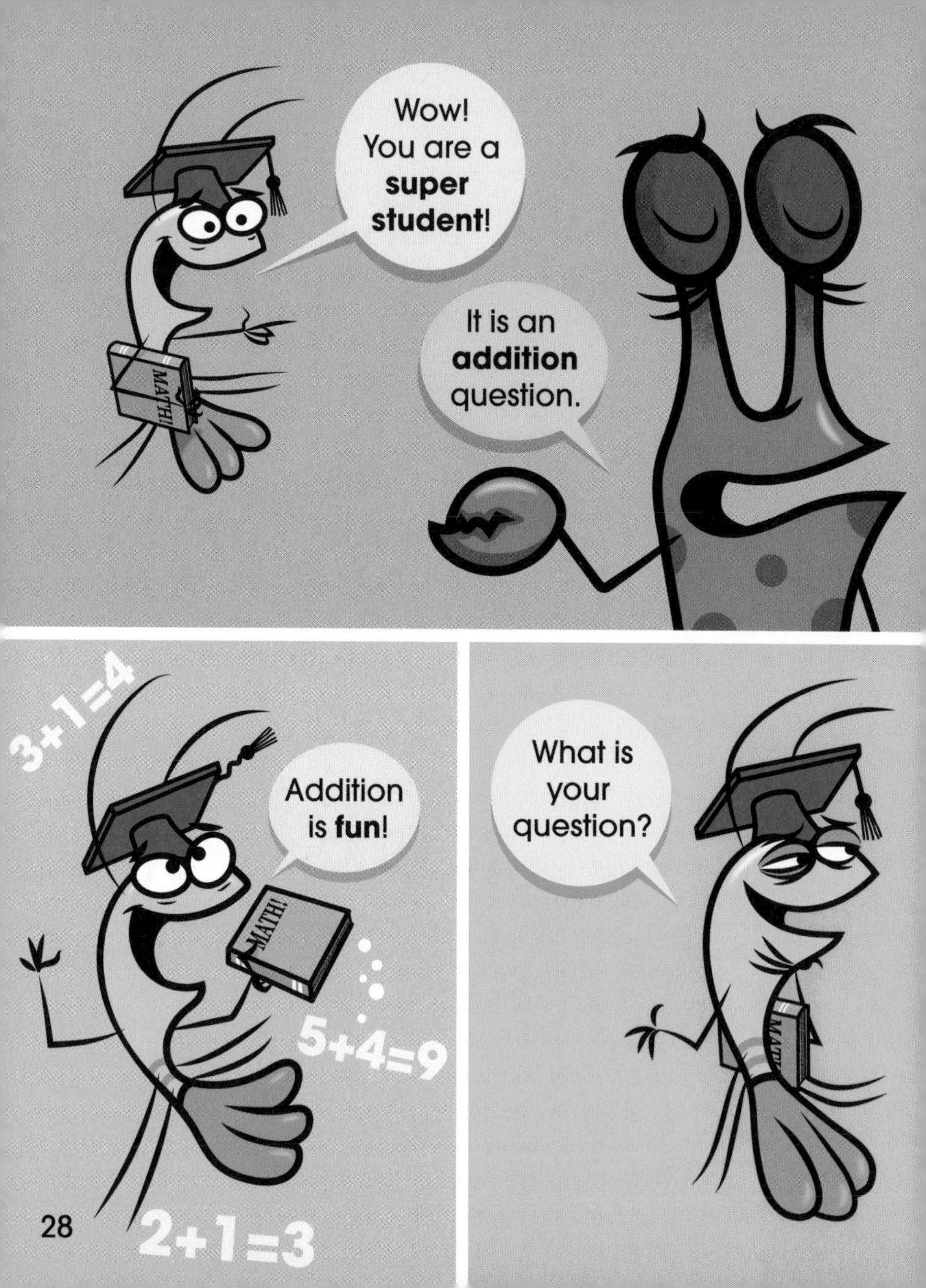
Wow! You are a **super student**!
MATH!
It is an **addition** question.
3+1=4
Addition is **fun**!
MATH!
5+4=9
2+1=3
What is your question?
MATH!

29

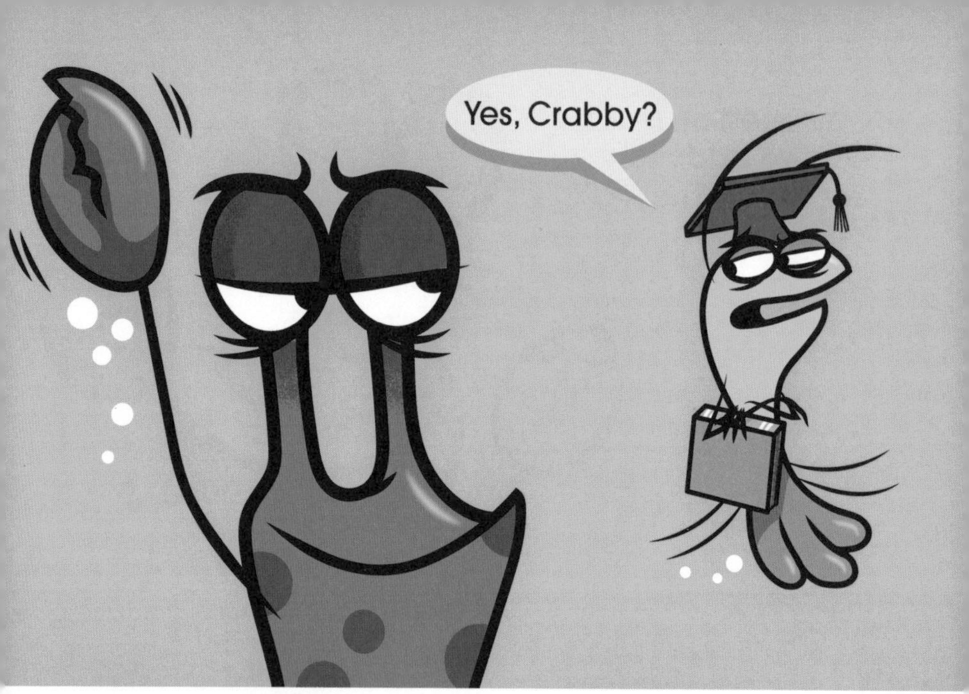
Yes, Crabby?

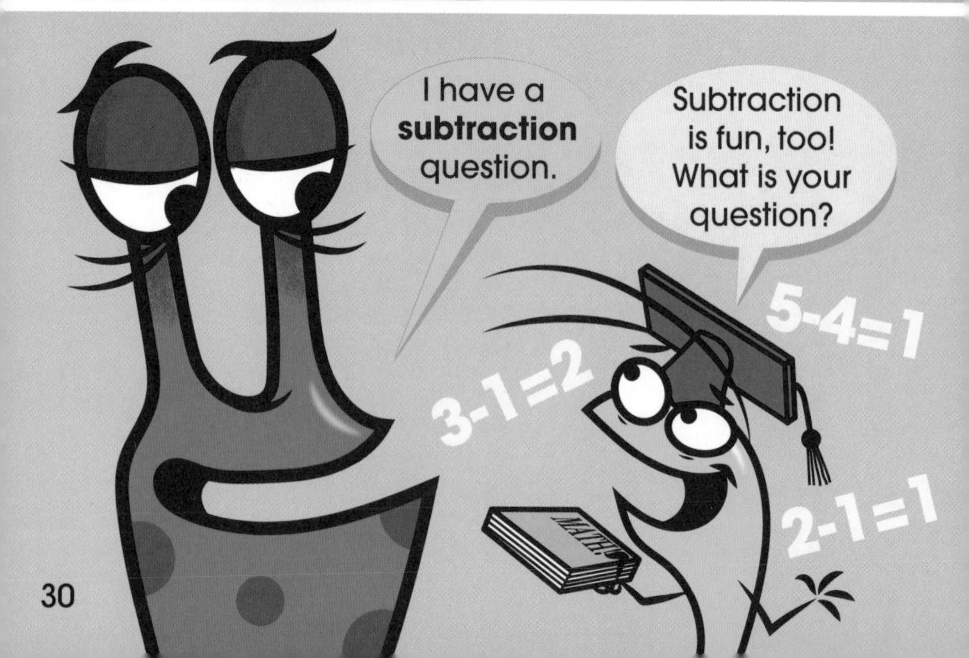
I have a **subtraction** question.
Subtraction is fun, too! What is your question?
5-4=1
3-1=2
2-1=1
MATH!

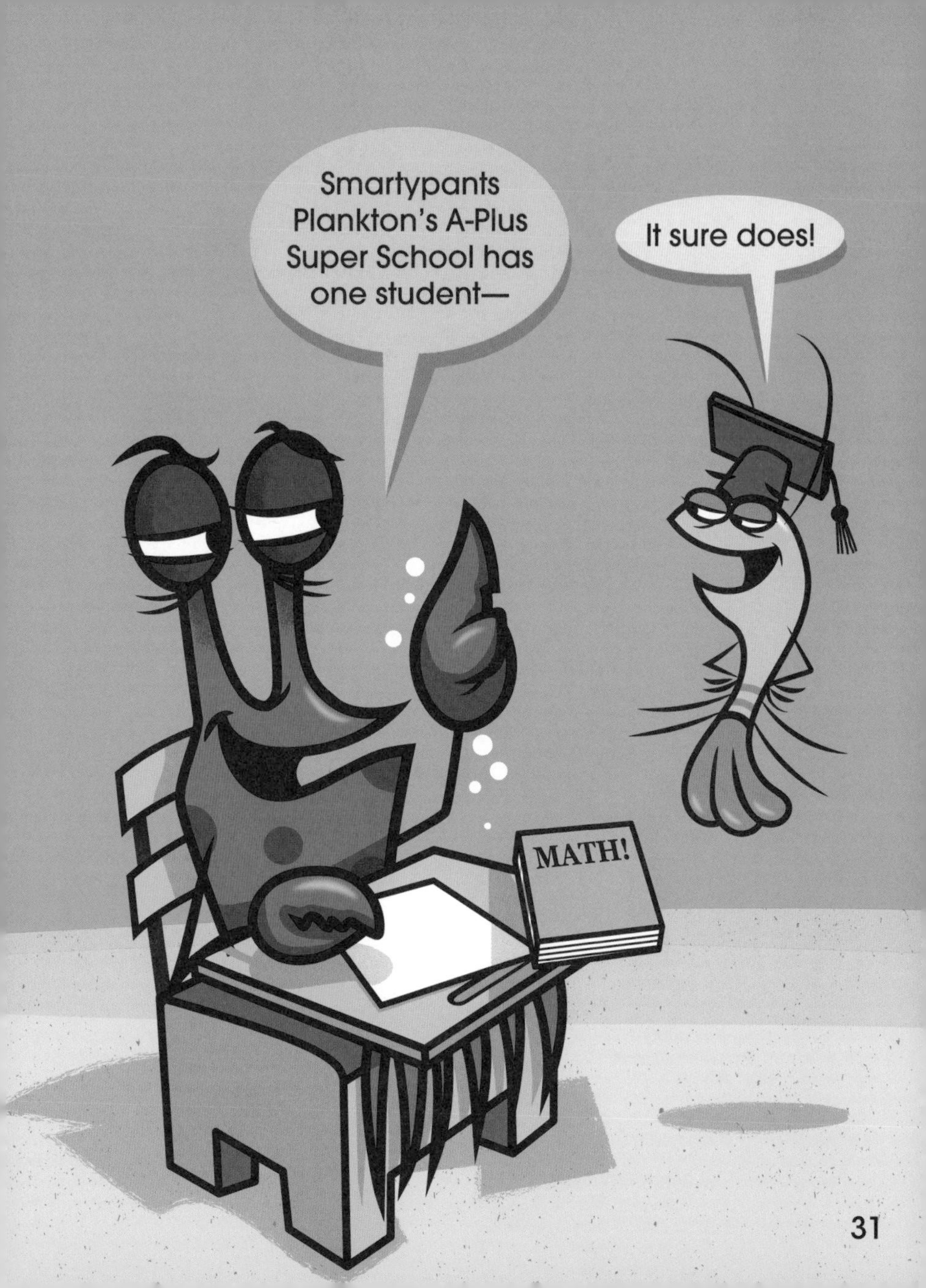
Smartypants Plankton's A-Plus Super School has one student—
It sure does!
MATH!

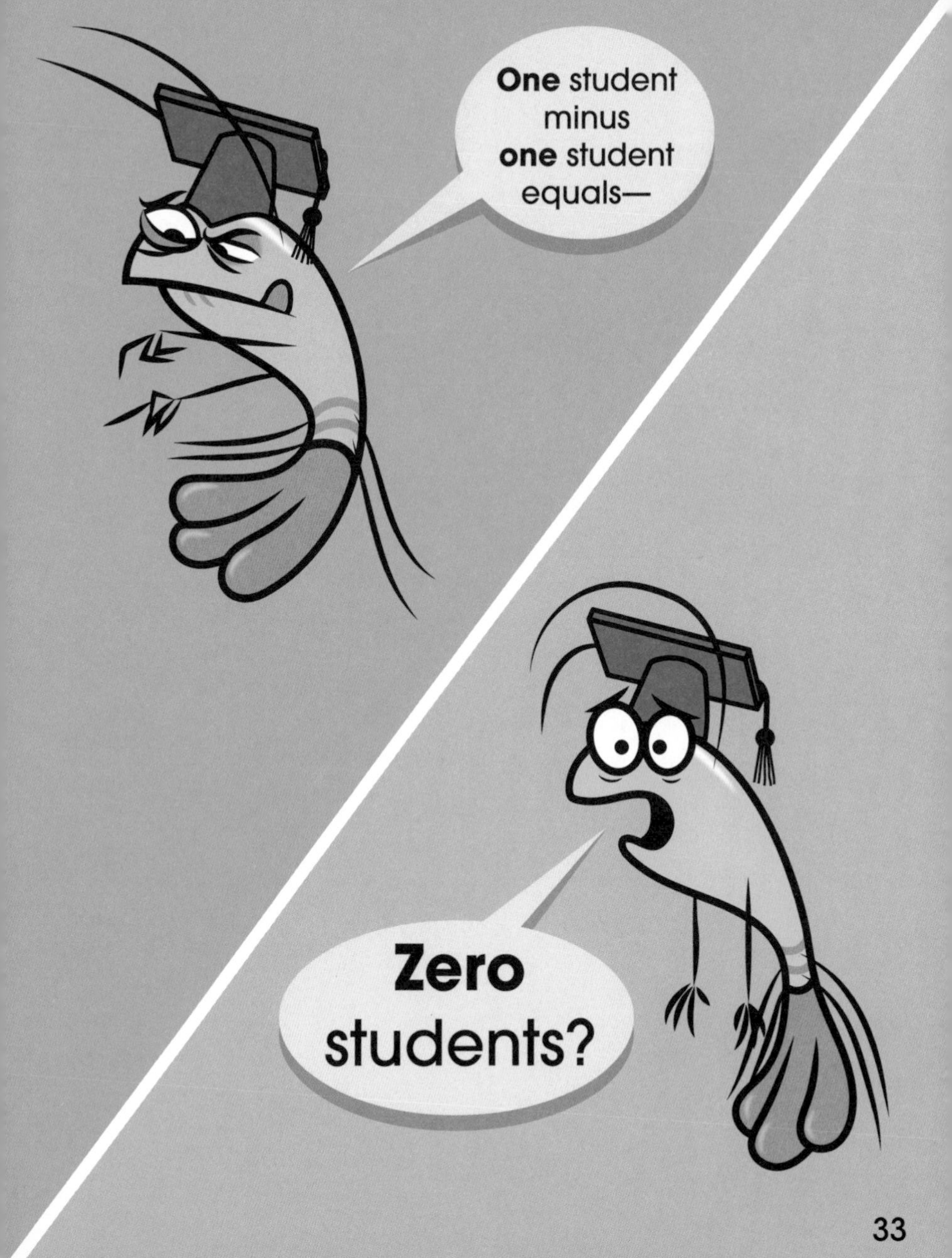
One student minus **one** student equals—
Zero students?

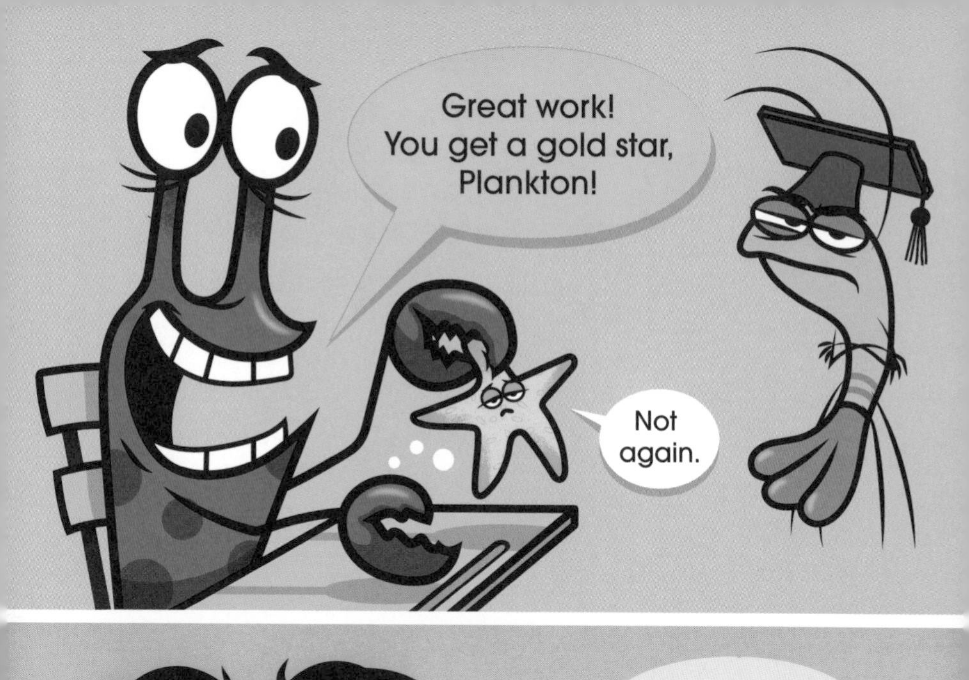
Great work! You get a gold star, Plankton!
Not again.
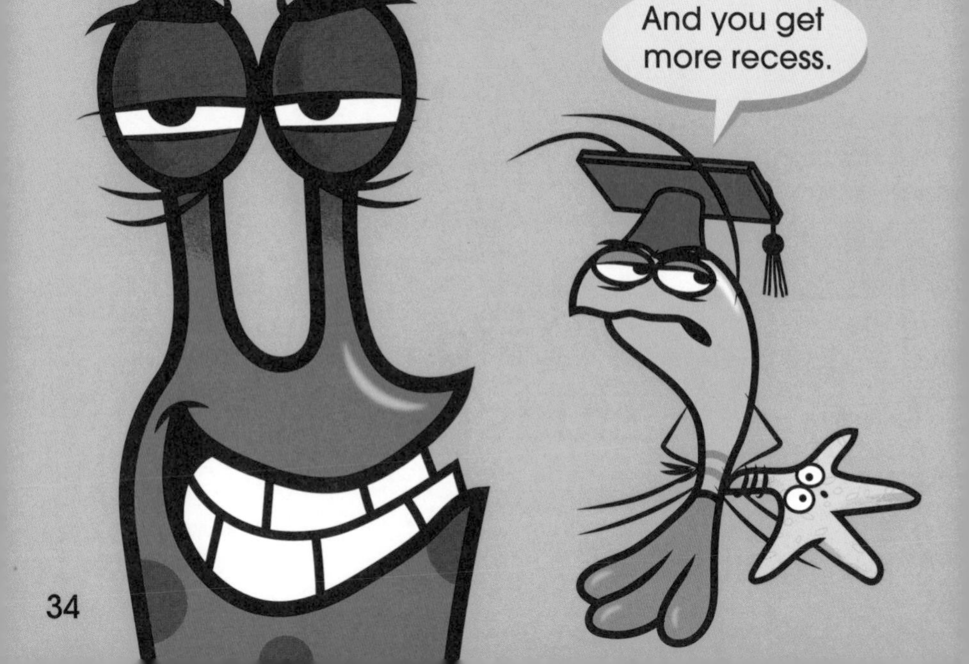
And you get more recess.

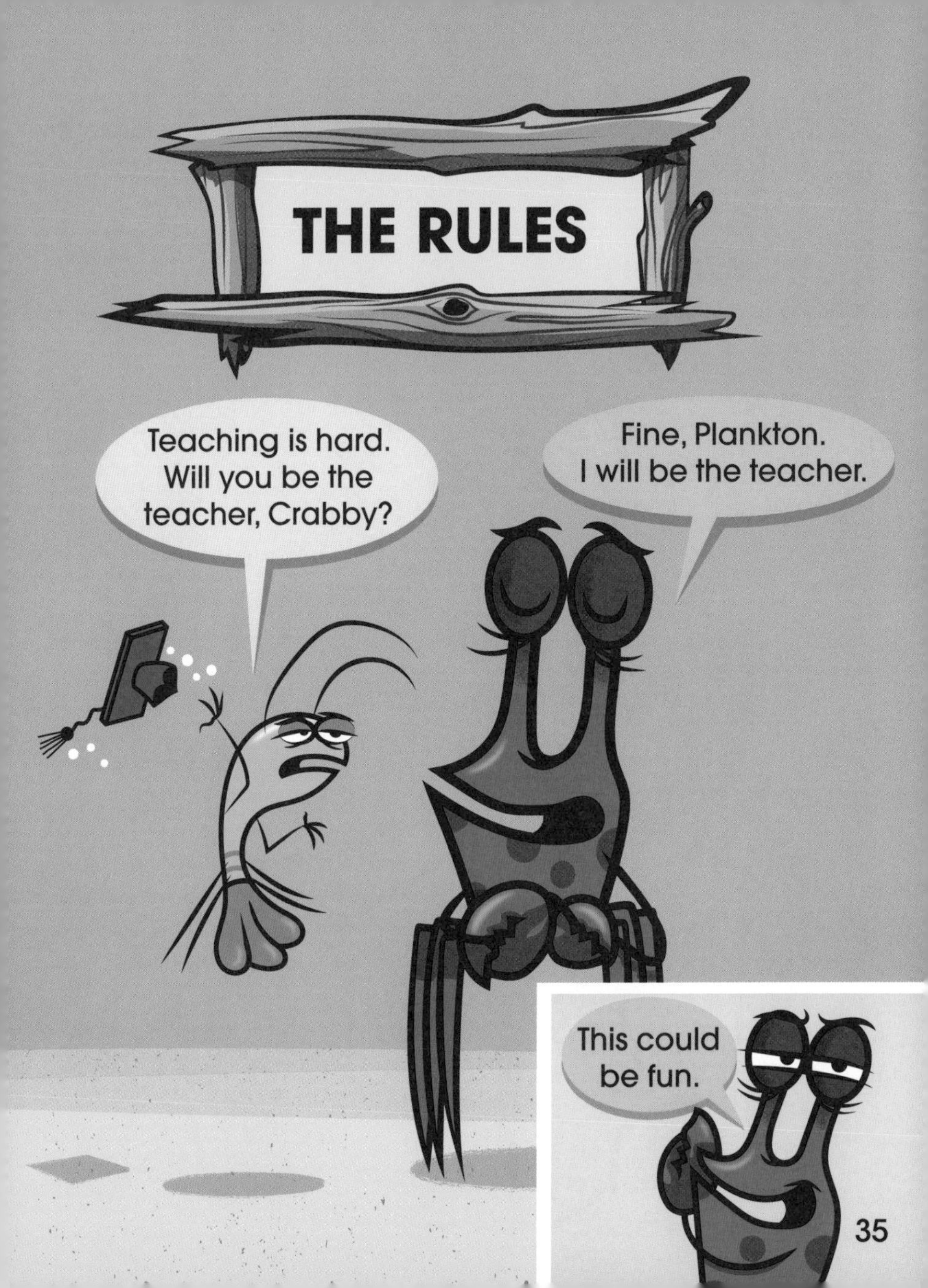
THE RULES
Teaching is hard. Will you be the teacher, Crabby?
Fine, Plankton. I will be the teacher.
This could be fun.

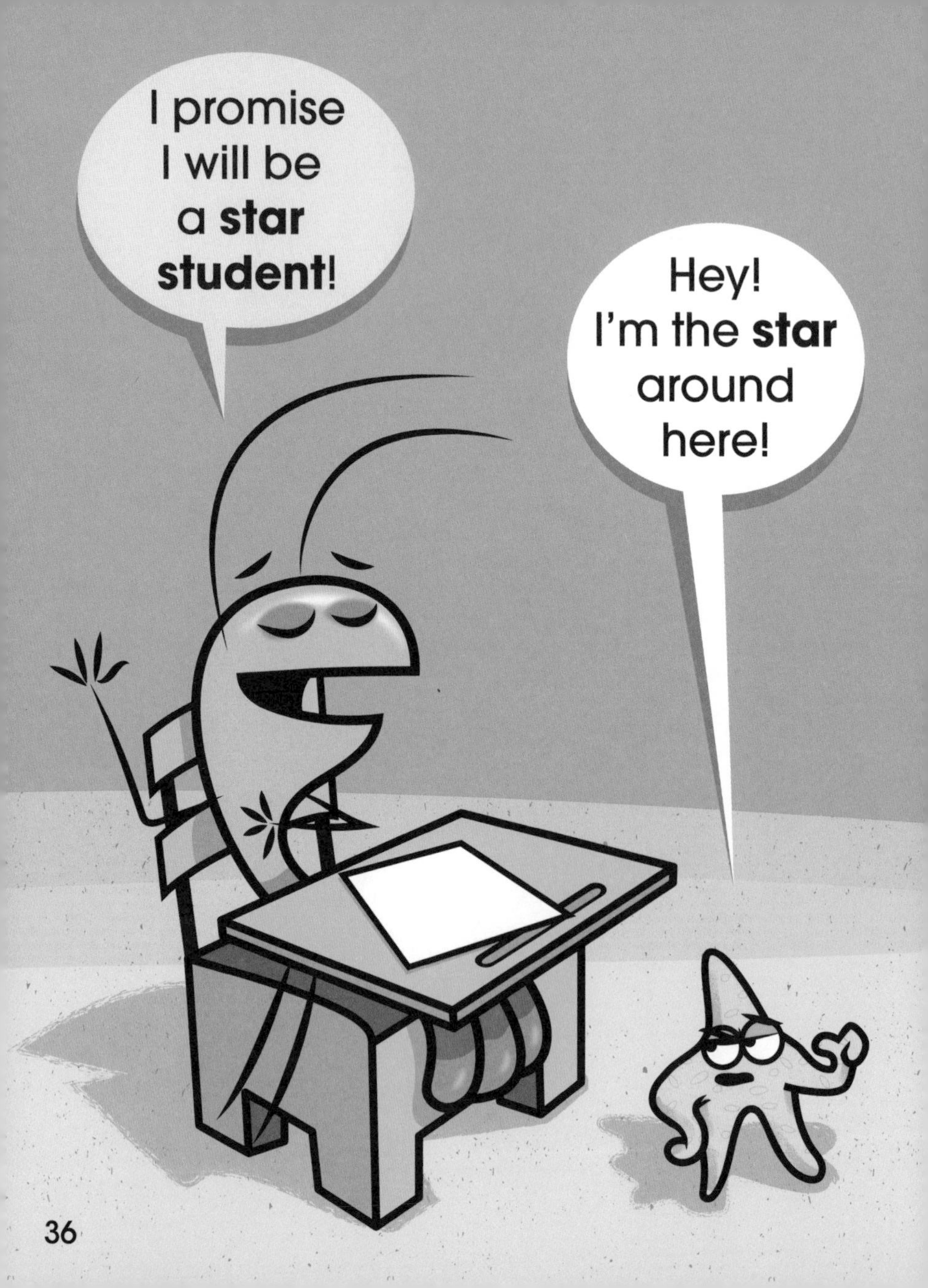
I promise I will be a **star student**!
Hey! I'm the **star** around here!

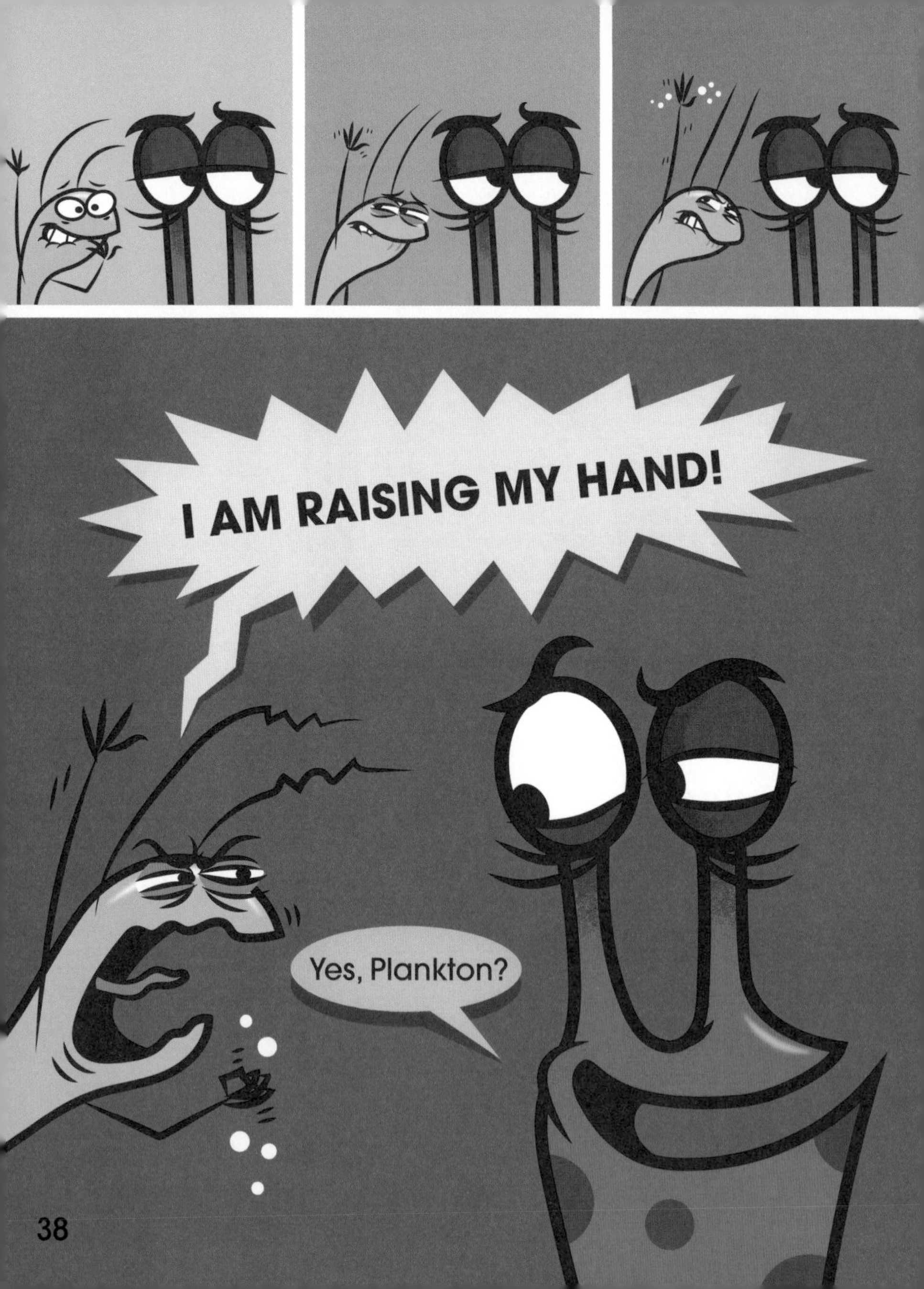

I AM RAISING MY HAND!

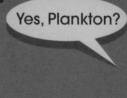

Yes, Plankton?

39

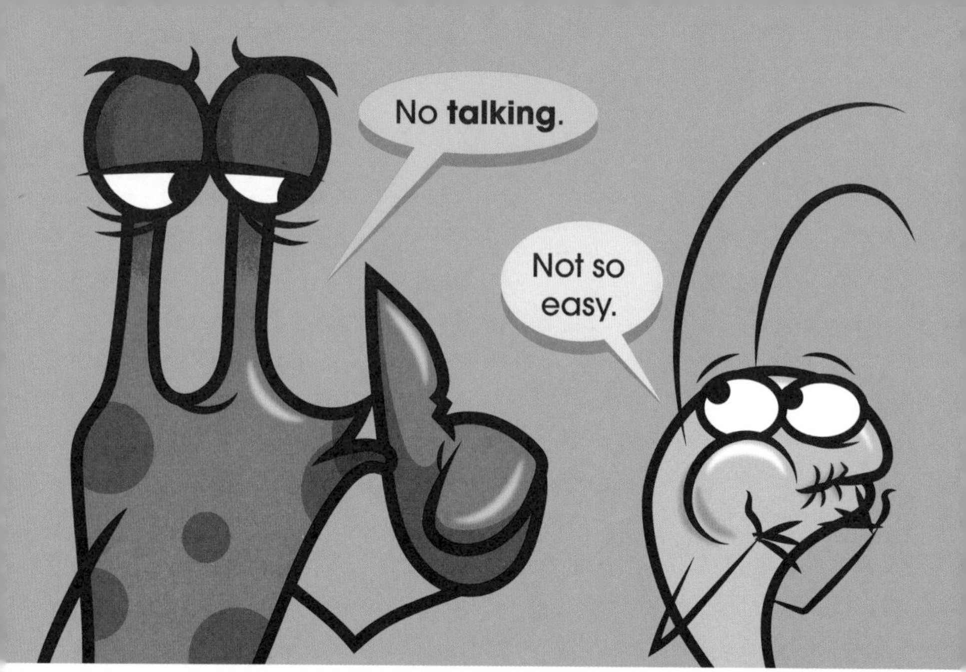
No **talking**.
Not so easy.

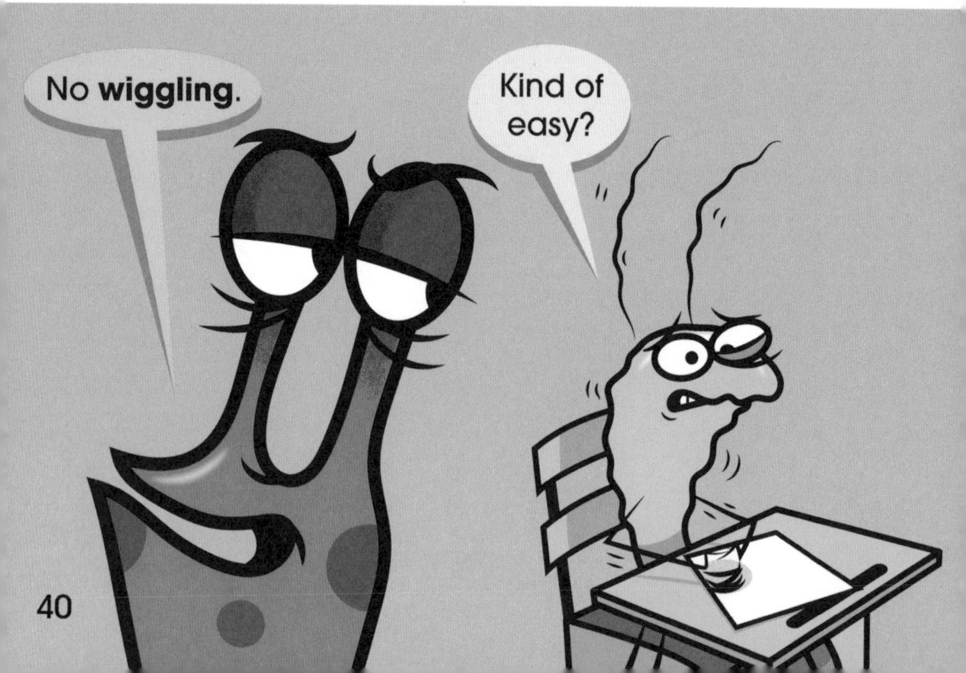
No **wiggling**.
Kind of easy?

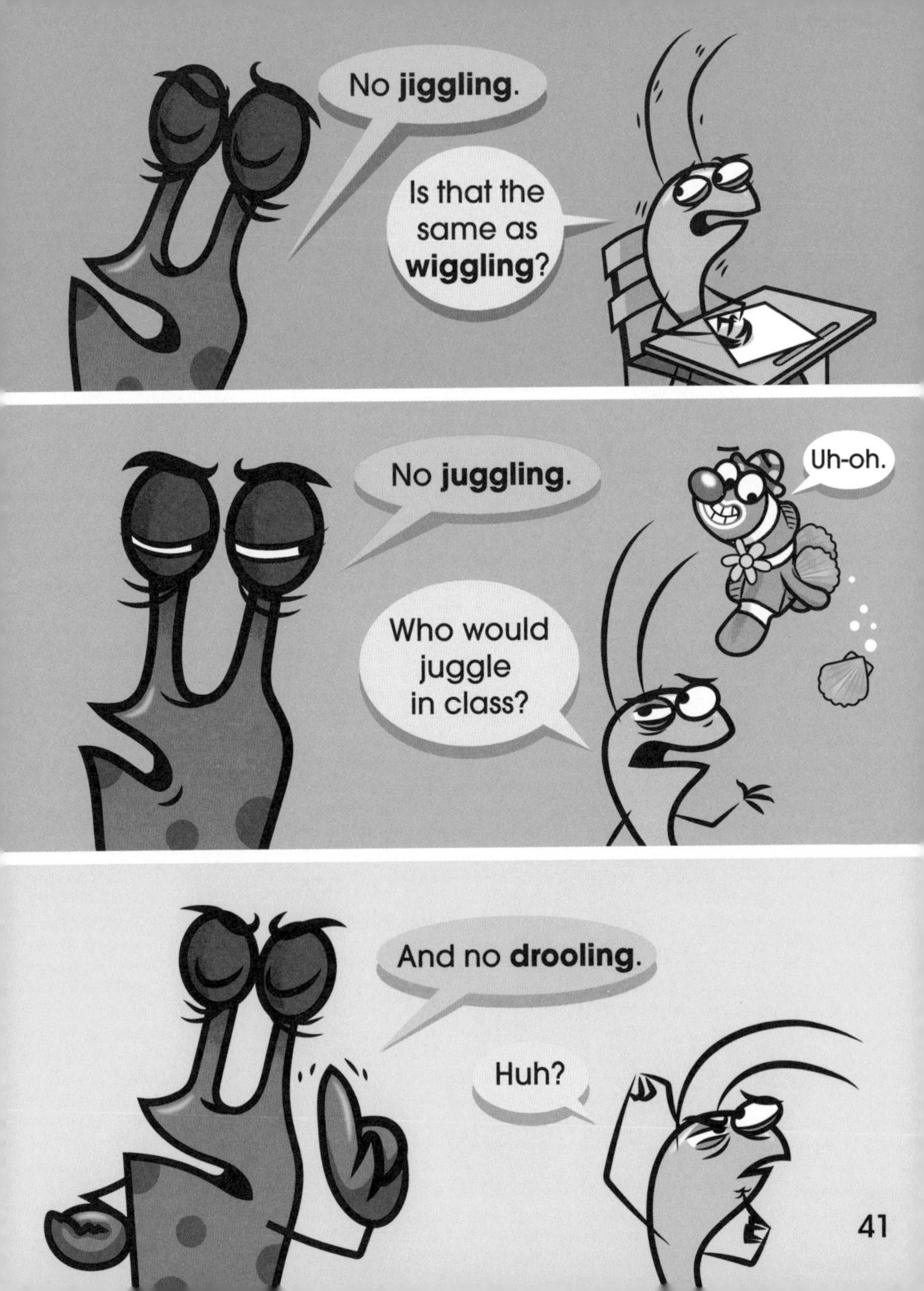
No **jiggling**.
Is that the same as **wiggling**?
No **juggling**.
Uh-oh.
Who would juggle in class?
And no **drooling**.
Huh?

43

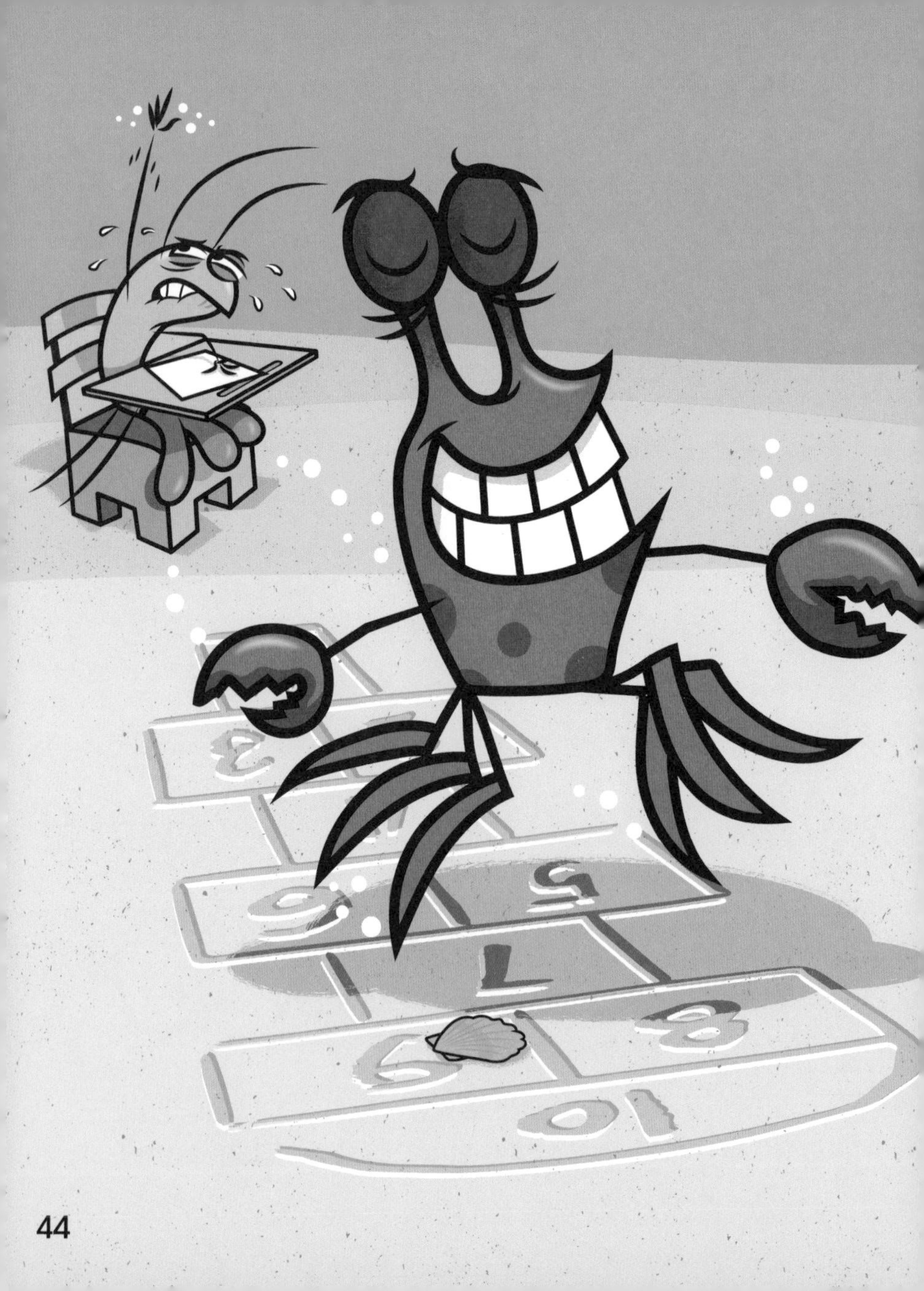

About the Author

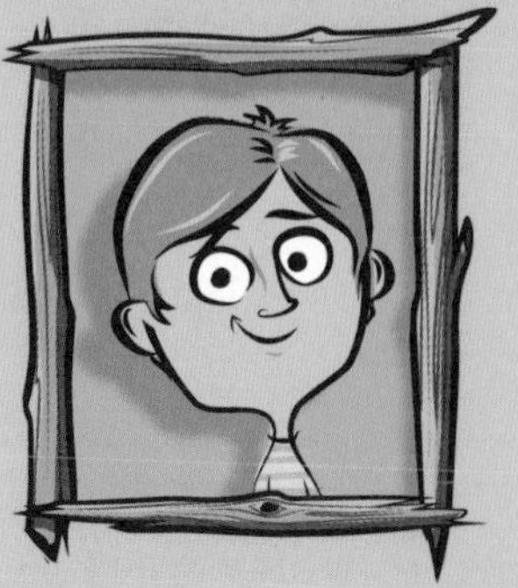

Jonathan Fenske lives in South Carolina with his family. He was born in Florida near the ocean, so he knows all about life at the beach! His favorite part of school was definitely recess!

Jonathan is the author and illustrator of several children's books including **Barnacle Is Bored**, **Plankton Is Pushy** (a Junior Library Guild selection), and **After Squidnight**. His early reader **A Pig, a Fox, and a Box** was a Theodor Seuss Geisel Honor Book.

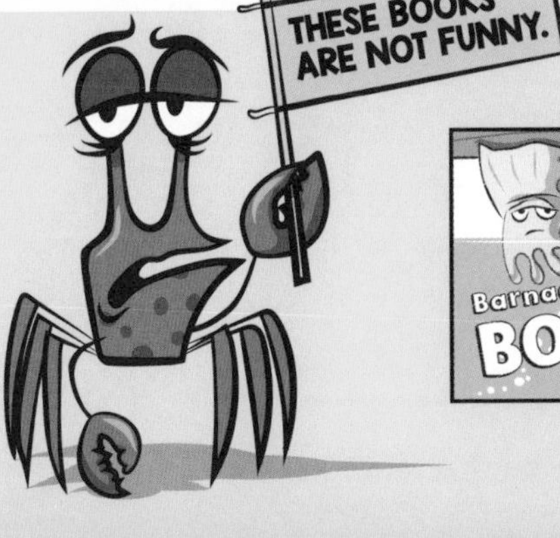
THESE BOOKS
ARE NOT FUNNY.

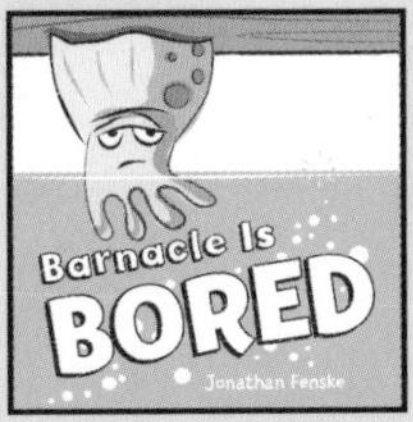
Barnacle Is
BORED
Jonathan Fenske

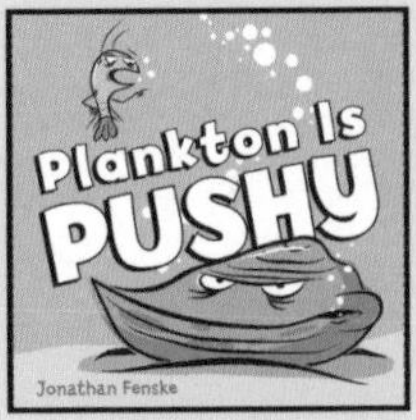
Plankton Is
PUSHY
Jonathan Fenske

YOU CAN DRAW FISHY!

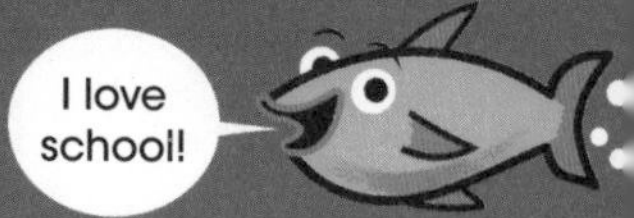
I love school!

1. Draw two curvy lines connected at the front.

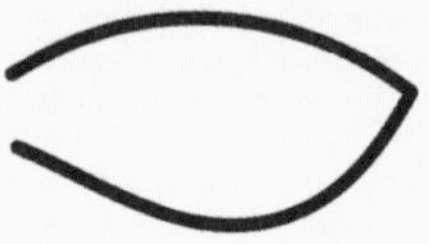

2. Close the shape with a tail.

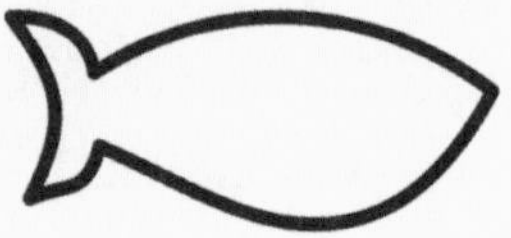

3. Add fins on the top, bottom, and side of the fish.

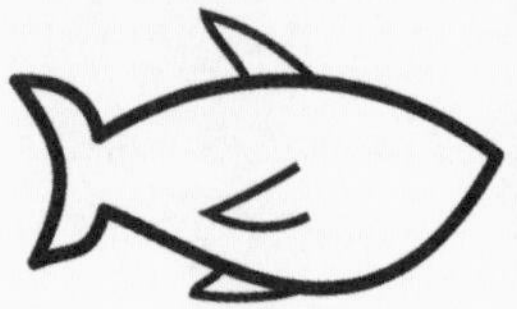

4. Draw the eye and mouth.

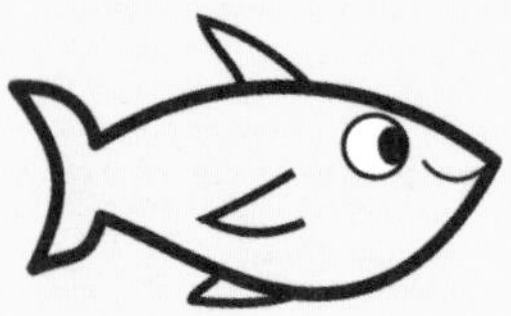

5. Color Fishy however you like. Don't forget the bubbles!

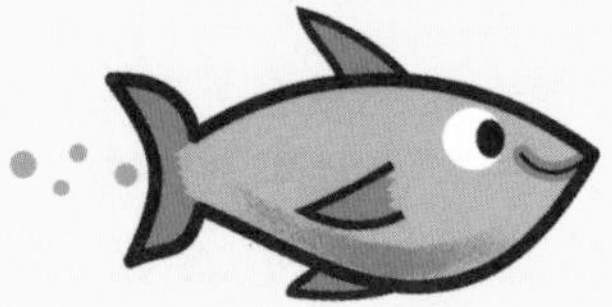

6. Draw several fish to make a school!

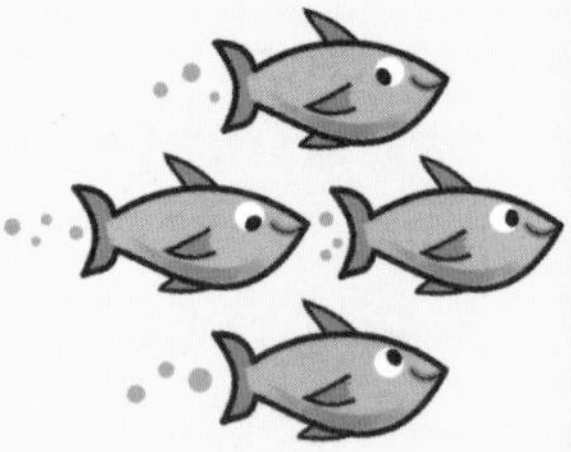

WHAT'S YOUR STORY?

Plankton and Crabby are playing school!
What do you do during the school day?
Would you want Plankton or Crabby to be your teacher?
Write and draw your story!

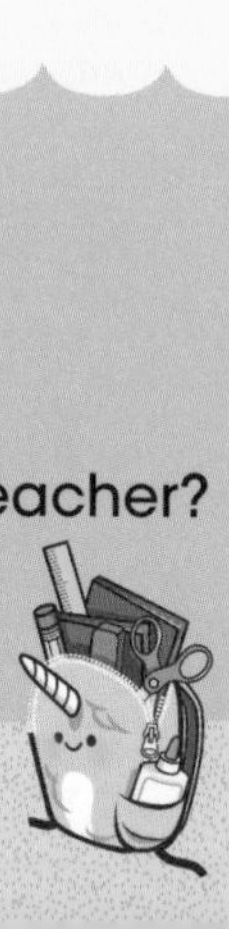